THE CASE OF THE
Crying Swallow

A PERRY MASON NOVELETTE
AND OTHER STORIES

Erle Stanley Gardner

The Case of the Crying Swallow

A Perry Mason Novelette and Other Stories

William Morrow and Company · New York

BOOKS BY ERLE STANLEY GARDNER

The Perry Mason Cases

THE CASE OF THE

VELVET CLAWS, 1933
SULKY GIRL, 1933
LUCKY LEGS, 1934
HOWLING DOG, 1934
CURIOUS BRIDE, 1934
COUNTERFEIT EYE, 1935
CARETAKER'S CAT, 1935
SLEEPWALKER'S NIECE, 1936
STUTTERING BISHOP, 1936
DANGEROUS DOWAGER, 1937
LAME CANARY, 1937
SUBSTITUTE FACE, 1938
SHOPLIFTER'S SHOE, 1938
PERJURED PARROT, 1939
ROLLING BONES, 1939
BAITED HOOK, 1940
SILENT PARTNER, 1940
HAUNTED HUSBAND, 1941
EMPTY TIN, 1941
DROWNING DUCK, 1942
CARELESS KITTEN, 1942
BURIED CLOCK, 1943
DROWSY MOSQUITO, 1943
CROOKED CANDLE, 1944
BLACK-EYED BLONDE, 1944
GOLDDIGGER'S PURSE, 1945
HALF-WAKENED WIFE, 1945
BORROWED BRUNETTE, 1946
FAN-DANCER'S HORSE, 1947
LAZY LOVER, 1947
LONELY HEIRESS, 1948
VAGABOND VIRGIN, 1948
DUBIOUS BRIDEGROOM, 1949
CAUTIOUS COQUETTE, 1949
NEGLIGENT NYMPH, 1950
ONE-EYED WITNESS, 1951
FIERY FINGERS, 1951
ANGRY MOURNER, 1951
MOTH-EATEN MINK, 1952
GRINNING GORILLA, 1952

HESITANT HOSTESS, 1953
GREEN-EYED SISTER, 1953
FUGITIVE NURSE, 1954
RUNAWAY CORPSE, 1954
RESTLESS REDHEAD, 1954
GLAMOROUS GHOST, 1955
SUN BATHER'S DIARY, 1955
NERVOUS ACCOMPLICE, 1955
TERRIFIED TYPIST, 1956
DEMURE DEFENDANT, 1956
GILDED LILY, 1956
LUCKY LOSER, 1957
SCREAMING WOMAN, 1957
DARING DECOY, 1957
LONG-LEGGED MODELS, 1958
FOOT-LOOSE DOLL, 1958
CALENDAR GIRL, 1958
DEADLY TOY, 1959
MYTHICAL MONKEYS, 1959
SINGING SKIRT, 1959
WAYLAID WOLF, 1960
DUPLICATE DAUGHTER, 1960
SHAPELY SHADOW, 1960
SPURIOUS SPINSTER, 1961
BIGAMOUS SPOUSE, 1961
RELUCTANT MODEL, 1962
BLONDE BONANZA, 1962
ICE-COLD HANDS, 1962
MISCHIEVOUS DOLL, 1963
STEPDAUGHTER'S SECRET, 1963
AMOROUS AUNT, 1963
DARING DIVORCEE, 1964
PHANTOM FORTUNE, 1964
HORRIFIED HEIRS, 1964
TROUBLED TRUSTEE, 1965
BEAUTIFUL BEGGAR, 1965
WORRIED WAITRESS, 1966
QUEENLY CONTESTANT, 1967
CARELESS CUPID, 1968
FABULOUS FAKE, 1969
CRIMSON KISS, 1970

"The king of the mystery field" * is also the author of:

THE CLUE OF THE FORGOTTEN
  MURDER, 1935
THIS IS MURDER, 1935
THE D.A. CALLS IT MURDER, 1937
MURDER UP MY SLEEVE, 1938
THE D.A. HOLDS A CANDLE, 1938
THE BIGGER THEY COME, 1939
THE D.A. DRAWS A CIRCLE, 1939
TURN ON THE HEAT, 1940
THE D.A. GOES TO TRIAL, 1940
GOLD COMES IN BRICKS, 1940
THE CASE OF THE
  TURNING TIDE, 1941
SPILL THE JACKPOT!, 1941
DOUBLE OR QUITS, 1941
THE D.A. COOKS A GOOSE, 1942
OWLS DON'T BLINK, 1942
BATS FLY AT DUSK, 1942
THE CASE OF THE
  SMOKING CHIMNEY, 1943
CATS PROWL AT NIGHT, 1943
THE D.A. CALLS A TURN, 1944
GIVE 'EM THE AX, 1944
THE CASE OF THE BACKWARD
  MULE, 1946
THE D.A. BREAKS THE SEAL, 1946
CROWS CAN'T COUNT, 1946
TWO CLUES: THE CLUE OF THE
  RUNAWAY BLONDE AND THE
  CLUE OF THE HUNGRY HORSE,
  1947
FOOLS DIE ON FRIDAY, 1947
THE D.A. TAKES A CHANCE, 1948
BEDROOMS HAVE WINDOWS, 1949
THE D.A. BREAKS AN EGG, 1949
THE CASE OF THE MUSICAL COW,
  1950
TOP OF THE HEAP, 1952
SOME WOMEN WON'T WAIT,
  1953

BEWARE THE CURVES, 1956
YOU CAN DIE LAUGHING, 1957
SOME SLIPS DON'T SHOW, 1957
THE COUNT OF NINE, 1958
PASS THE GRAVY, 1959
KEPT WOMEN CAN'T QUIT, 1960
BACHELORS GET LONELY, 1961
SHILLS CAN'T CASH CHIPS, 1961
TRY ANYTHING ONCE, 1962
FISH OR CUT BAIT, 1963
UP FOR GRABS, 1964
CUT THIN TO WIN, 1965
WIDOWS WEAR WEEDS, 1966
TRAPS NEED FRESH BAIT, 1967
ALL GRASS ISN'T GREEN, 1970

NON FICTION

THE LAND OF SHORTER
  SHADOWS, 1948
THE COURT OF LAST RESORT,
  1952
NEIGHBORHOOD FRONTIERS,
  1954
HUNTING THE DESERT WHALE,
  1960
HOVERING OVER BAJA, 1961
THE HIDDEN HEART OF BAJA,
  1962
THE DESERT IS YOURS, 1963
THE WORLD OF WATER, 1964
HUNTING LOST MINES
  BY HELICOPTER, 1965
OFF THE BEATEN TRACK
  IN BAJA, 1967
GYPSY DAYS ON THE DELTA,
  1967
MEXICO'S MAGIC SQUARE, 1968
HOST WITH THE BIG HAT, 1969
COPS ON CAMPUS AND CRIME
  IN THE STREETS, 1970

* *The Case of Erle Stanley Gardner,* by Alva Johnston. William Morrow & Co.,
Inc., 1947.

Publisher's Note

THIS is the second book by Erle Stanley Gardner to be published since his death in 1970.

The keynote of this volume is a novelette starring Perry Mason. Two of the short stories feature serial characters as well known to Gardner's magazine fans as Mason to his book audience: Lester Leith and Sidney Zoom. The third short story has a hero, who has appeared in just two of Gardner's stories—Jerry Bane, a self-appointed detective exemplary of his creator's quick wittedness and fast footwork.

The assortment adds up to a collection of gems—a statement that can be taken literally as well as figuratively, since the springboard for each story concerns stolen jewelry. This choice was deliberate to show how a truly inventive mind improvises ingenious variations on a theme. Barring one exception, no two stories are alike; they are so different in motivation, background, and characterization it is doubtful the absorbed reader would notice a common denominator, or think it relevant.

As to the exception, there is a parallel of note in two of the stories: The first appearance of Lester Leith was back in 1929 when Raffles was more than a memory and Philo Vance the

rage. Leith has captured the attention of the police not only
because of his uncanny ability to solve crimes but because
of his mysterious means of support for a highly Sybaritic way
of life. They have seen to it that his valet is a cop, planted to
spy on this latter-day Robin Hood. In 1940 Jerry Bane steps
from the wings. Jerry's parents prudently left his legacy in
trust since he had extravagant tastes and no prediliction for
gainful employment. Jerry also has a Man Friday, an ex-cop
whose loyalty to his young employer is equaled only by his
enduring memory for pedigrees of the underworld and its
periphery.

There is a gulf of time between the creation of these characters, a decade of enormous change, which Gardner with
characteristic alertness and vigor kept pace with and reflected
in his writing, thus effectively blotting any suggestion of repe-
tition or of dipping into the bin. Rather, the parallel empha-
sizes once more a unique writer's ability to improvise on a
theme.

The basic purpose, however, of any collection of detective
stories is entertainment for the reader—entertainment here
supplied by the incomparable Maestro of Mysteries, Erle
Stanley Gardner.

Contents

The Case of the Crying Swallow

CHAPTER ONE

PERRY MASON, tilted back in his walnut desk chair, was studying a recent decision of the state supreme court when Della Street, his secretary, opened the door from the outer office, advanced to the desk and quietly laid ten crisp one-hundred-dollar bills on the blotter.

Mason, too engrossed to notice what she was doing, continued his reading.

Della Street said, "A client sends his card."

Mason straightened in the swivel chair and for the first time caught sight of the money which Della Street had so neatly spread out.

"He said his name was Mr. Cash," Della Street explained. "Then he handed me ten one-hundred-dollar bills and said these were his cards."

Mason grinned. "So the black market begins to turn yellow. What does Mr. Cash look like?"

"He's a floor walker."

Mason raised his eyebrows, glanced at the cash. "A *floor-walker?*"

"No, no, not a department store floorwalker! I mean that he's a floor *walker,* the same as you are. He paces the floor when he's worried. He's doing a carpet marathon out there right now."

Mason said, "I don't know whether civilization is breaking down the character of our criminals or whether the black market operators haven't been in business long enough to develop intestinal stamina. The bootleggers were a tougher breed. My own opinion is that these black market operators simply haven't had time to become accustomed to the fact that they're on the other side of society's legal fence. Give them another eighteen months and they'll be as tough as the old gangsters."

"He definitely *isn't* a black market operator," Della Street said positively. "He's distinguished-looking, has a slight limp, is deeply tanned and . . . and I've seen him somewhere before. Oh, now I have it. I've seen his picture!"

"Give."

"Major Claude L. Winnett, polo player, yachtsman, millionaire playboy. When the war came, he quit being a playboy and became an aviator, bagged a whole flock of German planes and then was captured, liberated last fall, discharged because of his wound, returned to his doting mother and . . ."

Mason nodded. "I remember reading about the chap. He got a citation or something. Didn't he get married?"

"About four or five weeks ago," Della Street said. "That was where I first saw his picture—in the paper. Then again last week a reporter for the society supplement paid a visit to the Winnett home—one of the old-time country estates with stables of polo ponies, riding trails, hedges, private golf courses . . ."

"Show him in," Mason said. "But let him know first that you've placed him. It may save time."

Major Winnett, lean, fit, bronzed, and nervous, followed Della Street into the office. The excitement and anxiety of his manner were more noticeable than his slight limp. A well-modulated voice and patrician bearing made his surrender to emotion all the more impressive.

"Mr. Mason," he said as soon as he was in the room, "I had intended to keep my identity a secret and ask you to represent another person. Now that your secretary has recognized me, I'll put my cards on the table. My wife has disappeared. She needs your help. She's in trouble of some sort."

"Tell me about it," Mason said.

Major Winnett reached into his inside pocket, took out a folded piece of letter paper and handed it to Mason.

The lawyer opened the letter and read:

Claude, my darling, there are some things that I can't drag *you* into. I thought I had a way out, but I guess I didn't. Our happiness was such a beautiful thing. But beautiful things are always fragile. Don't worry about anything. I am responsible, and I am not going to let you suffer because of what you have done for me. Good-by, my darling.—MARCIA

"What does she mean by saying she's responsible and not letting you suffer because of what you have done for her?" Mason asked.

Major Winnett's manner was uneasy. "My marriage was not exactly in accordance with the wishes of my mother. I went ahead with it despite her objections."

"Spoken objections?"

"Certainly not."

"Yet your wife knew of them?"

"Women feel many things without the necessity of words, Mr. Mason. I want you to find her and straighten things out for her."

"And then report to you?"

"Certainly."

Mason shook his head.

For a moment there was silence, broken only by the
faint rumble of traffic and the breathing of Mason's client.
Then Major Winnett said, "Very well. Do it your way."

"When did your wife leave?"

"Last night. I found this note on the dresser about midnight. I thought she had previously retired."

"Is there any reason why your wife would have been vulnerable to what we might call an outside influence?"

"Absolutely not—if you mean blackmail."

"Then tell me why your wife wasn't free to come to you
with her troubles."

"I don't know, unless it's on account of my mother."

"What about her?"

"My mother is a very unusual person. When my father
died, a dozen years ago, Mother stepped in and took charge.
She is living in a bygone era. She has old-fashioned ideas."

"The proprieties?" Mason asked.

"Not so much the proprieties as . . . well, class distinc-
tions, the aristocracy of wealth and that sort of thing. I think
she would have been happier if I had married someone
more in our own set."

"Who, for instance?"

"Oh, I didn't say any particular person," Major Winnett
said hastily.

"I know you didn't. That's why I'm asking you."

"Well, perhaps Daphne Rexford."

"You think this caused your wife to leave?"

"No, no. Not directly. My mother has accepted Marcia into
the family. Whatever may have been Mother's ideas about
the marriage, Marcia is now one of us—a Winnett."

"Then suppose you tell me what you mean when you say
'not directly.' "

"Marcia would have done anything rather than subject me
to any notoriety because she knew how my mother felt about

THE CASE OF THE CRYING SWALLOW

that. You see, Mr. Mason, we live in a large, rather old-fashioned estate surrounded by hedges, with our private bridle paths, high wire fences, locked gates, no-trespassing signs and all the rest. The more the world moves in a way that meets with the disapproval of my mother, the more she tries to shut that part of the world out from her life."

"Anything unusual happen within the last few days?" the lawyer asked, probing his client's mind.

"A burglar entered our house Tuesday night."

"Take anything?" Mason asked.

"My wife's jewelry, valued at perhaps twenty-five or thirty thousand dollars, although I don't suppose a person could get that for it. It had been insured at fifteen thousand dollars."

"Had been?" Mason asked.

"Yes, my wife canceled the insurance. As it happened, only the day before the burglary."

Major Winnett glanced almost appealingly at the lawyer.

"Canceled her insurance," Mason said, "and then twenty-four hours later the burglary took place?"

"Yes."

"And you fail to see any connection between those two facts?"

"I am certain there is none," Major Winnett said hastily. "My wife's reasoning was absolutely sound. She had carried this insurance policy and paid high premiums on it while she was living in apartments and hotels because she wanted to keep her jewelry with her and wanted to wear it. But when she married me and came to live in Vista del Mar, it seemed hardly necessary to continue paying high premiums."

"Tell me more about that burglary and why you didn't report it to the police."

"How did you know we didn't report it to the police?"

"Your facial expression," Mason said dryly.

"That was purely on account of the fact that my mother
. . . well, you know, the newspaper notoriety and . . ."

"Tell me about the burglary," Mason said.

Major Winnett spoke with the rhythm of a man who is carefully choosing his words. "I am a sound sleeper, Mr. Mason.
My wife is not. On Tuesday night I was awakened by the
sound of my wife's scream."

"What time?"

"I didn't look at my watch at the time but I did look at it
a few minutes later, and as nearly as I can place the time, it
was around quarter to one."

"How long had you been in bed?"

"We retired about eleven."

"And you slept until your wife screamed?"

"Well, I have, in the back of my consciousness, a vague
recollection of a swallow crying."

Mason raised his eyebrows.

"You are, of course, familiar," Major Winnett went
on hastily, "with the famed swallows of the Mission of San
Juan Capistrano?"

Mason nodded.

"The nesting place of those swallows is not confined to the
Mission. They get more publicity at the Mission because they
leave on a certain day and return on a certain day. I believe
that the time of their return can be predicted almost to the
hour. A very unusual sense of keeping a calendar. How they
are able to return year after year . . ."

"And you have some of those swallows at your house?"
Mason interrupted.

"Yes. They are a nuisance. Their nests are built out of mud
and are fastened to the eaves. Our gardener knocks them
down as soon as he detects the birds building, but in case one
of them eludes his vigilance and the nest is built, then we

don't disturb it, because the birds lay eggs very soon after the nests are built."

"Go on," Mason said.

"Well, this particular swallow's nest was located in a very unfortunate place. The main residence at Vista del Mar is a large Spanish-type house with the tile roofs and a white exterior. Our bedroom is on the second floor with a projecting balcony. The tile projects out over that balcony, and the birds had made their nest in such a place that if a man climbed over the balcony rail, he'd be within a few feet of the nest."

"And a man did climb over that rail?"

"Evidently that is what happened. We found a ladder that had been placed against the side of the house. The intruder had climbed up the ladder. In doing so, he disturbed the swallows. When they're disturbed, they have a peculiar throaty chirp."

"And you heard that?"

"I either heard it or dreamed that I did. My wife doesn't remember it, and she is a much lighter sleeper than I am, but I don't think I was mistaken."

"Then you went back to sleep?"

"Apparently I did. I remember hearing the protestations of the swallows but, although I was aroused from a sound slumber, I didn't thoroughly waken. I dozed off again and was soon in a deep sleep from which I was awakened by my wife's scream."

"She saw the burglar?"

"She was aroused by some noise in the room. She saw this man standing at her dresser. At first she thought I had gone to the dresser for some purpose and she started to speak to me. Then she looked over and saw that I was in my bed . . ."

"There was enough light for that?"

"Yes. A late moon was giving some light."

"What happened?"

"The man heard the motion—some sound of the bed-springs, I guess. He darted out to the balcony. My wife screamed and that wakened me, but it took me a few seconds to get oriented, to realize where I was and what was happening. By that time the man had made his escape."

"And you think the swallows were crying because the man disturbed them?"

"That's right. When he entered the building, he must have climbed over the balcony rail and touched the nest."

"When did your wife cancel the insurance?"

"Monday afternoon."

Mason toyed with his lead pencil, then asked abruptly, "What happened Monday morning?"

"We all four breakfasted together."

"Who's the fourth?"

"Helen Custer, my mother's nurse."

"Your mother isn't well?"

"She has a bad heart. Her physician feels it's advisable to have a nurse in the house."

"She's been with you long?"

"For three years. We consider her very much one of the family."

"You breakfasted and then what?"

"I wrote letters. My mother . . . I don't know exactly where she *did* go. Marcia went riding."

"Where?"

"Heavens, I don't know. One of our bridle paths."

Mason said, "I believe it rained Sunday night, didn't it?"

Major Winnett looked at him curiously. "What," he asked, "does that have to do with it? . . . I mean, what is the significance?"

"Skip it," Mason interrupted. "What happened next?"

"Nothing. My wife returned about eleven."

"When did she tell you she was going to cancel the insurance?"

"That was just before lunch. She telephoned to the insurance company, and then she wrote them a letter confirming her action."

"Did you notice anything unusual in your wife's manner?"

"Nothing," Major Winnett said so swiftly that it seemed the answer had been poised on his tongue, waiting merely for Mason's question.

Mason said, "Well, it's ten-thirty. I want to get Paul Drake of the Drake Detective Agency. We'll make a start out at your place and go on from there. I'll leave here about eleven. Does your mother know your wife has left?"

Major Winnett cleared his throat. "I told her my wife was visiting friends."

"How will you account for us?" Mason asked.

"How many will there be?"

"My secretary, Miss Street, Paul Drake, the detective, myself, and perhaps one of Mr. Drake's assistants."

Major Winnett said, "I'm working on a mining deal. I can explain to my mother that you're giving me some advice in connection with that. Your detective wouldn't mind posing as a mining expert?"

"Not at all."

"You'll come to the house and . . . will you want to stay there?"

Mason nodded. "I think we'd better. And I'll want photographs and a description of your wife."

Major Winnett took an envelope from his inside pocket and extracted nearly a dozen photographs. "I brought these along. They're snapshots. She's twenty-five, redheaded, bluish-gray eyes, five feet two, a hundred and fifteen, and as nearly as I can tell from checking the clothes that are left in the closet, she's wearing a checkered suit, sort of a gray plaid. It's the one that she's wearing in this picture."

Mason studied the photographs, then reached for the envelope. "All right," he said, "we'll be out. You can go on ahead and see that all necessary arrangements are made."

CHAPTER TWO

THE CITY of Silver Strand Beach lay in a sheltered cove on the lee side of a peninsula. The Winnett estate dominated this peninsula, its wire fences with forbidding no-trespassing signs stretching for some two and a half miles. The Spanish-type house, perched on the summit some five hundred feet above the ocean, commanded a view in all directions.

Mason's car swept around the last curve in the graveled driveway and came to a stop in front of the imposing house as he said to Paul Drake, "I think the cancellation of that insurance policy is, perhaps, the first indication of what she had in mind, Paul. And I think that may have some connection with the horseback ride she took Monday morning."

Paul Drake's professionally lugubrious face didn't change expression in the least. "Anything to go on, Perry?"

"It rained Sunday night," Mason said. "It hasn't rained since. If you could find the path she took, it's quite possible you might be able to track her horse."

"For the love of Pete, do I have to ride a horse?"

"Sure. Tell the groom you'd like to ride. Ask him about some of the bridle paths."

"I can't see anything from a horse," Drake complained. "When a horse trots, I bounce. When I bounce, I see double."

"After you get out of sight of the house, you can lead the horse," Mason suggested.

"How about me?" Della Street asked.

"Try to get acquainted with the nurse," Mason suggested, "and take a look around."

Major Winnett himself answered Mason's ring; and the swift efficiency with which he installed them in rooms, then introduced them to his mother and Helen Custer, the nurse, showed that he had already made his preliminary explanations.

When Drake departed for the stables, after having expressed his spurious enthusiasm for horseflesh, Major Winnett took Mason on a tour of inspection.

Once they were alone in the upper corridors, Major Winnett asked quickly and in a low voice, "Is there anything in particular you want to see?"

"I'd like to get familiar with the entire house," Mason said guardedly. "But you might begin by showing me *your* room."

Major Winnett's room was on the south side. Glass doors opened on the balcony, from which the ocean could be seen shimmering in the sunlight.

"That's the swallow's nest?" Mason asked, indicating a gourdlike projection of mud which extended from the tiles just above the balcony.

"That's the swallow's nest. You can see that a person climbing a ladder . . ."

"Was the ladder already there?" Mason asked.

"Yes. The handyman had been doing some work on a pane of glass on the side of the bedroom. He had left the ladder in position that night, because he intended to finish it the next morning. Damn careless of him."

"In that case," Mason said, "your thief was an opportunist, since he didn't bring his own ladder."

"Yes, I suppose so."

"One who was, moreover, apparently familiar with the house. How about your servants?"

"You can't ever tell," Major Winnett said. "Particularly these days. But I *think* they're all right. Mother pays good wages and most of the help have been with her for some time. However, she *is* rather strict at times and there is a certain turnover."

"You own virtually all of the land on this peninsula?"

"Quite a bit of it, but not all of it. In a moment we'll go up to the observation tower and I can show you around from there. Generally, we take in about three-fourths of the peninsula. There is a strip out on the end where the county maintains a public campground."

"The public can reach that camp without crossing your estate?"

"Yes. Our line runs along by the grove of trees—beautiful oaks that offer a place for picnics. Picnickers are always scattering papers and plates around. We try to persuade them to go on down to the public campgrounds on the end of the peninsula."

"So anyone who came out here at night would have been definitely a trespasser?"

"Quite definitely."

"And having taken that risk, must have had some specific objective in mind, and would, therefore, if he were at all prudent, have arranged some manner of reaching his objective?"

"Yes, I suppose so."

"Therefore," Mason went on, "either your burglar must have been someone who knew that the ladder was here, or else it was an inside job."

"But how could anyone have known the ladder was here?"

Mason said, "If you can see the camp and the picnic grounds from here, it is quite possible that someone in the camp or picnic grounds could see the house."

"Yes, the house is quite a landmark. You can see it for miles."

"And perhaps a man, looking up here about dusk and noticing that a ladder had been left in place, would have decided it might be worthwhile to climb that ladder."

"Yes, I suppose so. However, Mr. Mason, I can't see that there is the slightest connection between the theft of my wife's jewelry and her disappearance."

"Probably not," Mason said.

They finished their tour with a trip up a flight of stairs to the place which Major Winnett described as "the tower."

Here was a belfry-like room, fifteen feet square, with plate-glass windows on all sides. In the center, a pair of eighteen-power binoculars attached to a swivel on a tripod could be turned and locked in any position.

"In times past," Major Winnett explained, "when there was more merchant shipping up and down the coast, we used to enjoy looking the boats over. You see, these binoculars can be swung in any direction. Now I'll point them toward town and—"

"Just a minute," Mason warned sharply, as Major Winnett reached for the binoculars. "They seem to be pointed toward that grove of trees. If you don't mind, I'd like to look through them."

"Why, certainly. Help yourself."

Mason looked through the powerful prismatic binoculars. The right eye showed only a blur, but the left showed a shaded spot under the clump of big live oaks where the road crossed a mesa before dipping down through a little canyon to again come into view as it swung out toward the picnic and camping grounds on the extreme tip of the promontory.

"There's no central focusing screw," Major Winnett explained. "You have to adjust each eyepiece individually. Perhaps . . .

"Yes, so I see," Mason said, removing his eyes from the binoculars.

"Here is what I mean," Major Winnett went on. "You simply screw this eyepiece . . ."

Mason courteously but firmly arrested the major's hand. "Just a moment, Major," he said. "I want to look at that right eyepiece."

"Someone must have been tampering with it. It's way out of proper adjustment," the major said.

"The left eyepiece is at zero adjustment. I take it that means a perfectly normal eye," Mason said, "whereas, on this right eyepiece, there is an adjustment of negative five. I take it those graduations are made so that a person can remember his own individual adjustment for infinity and adjust the binoculars readily."

"I suppose so. The figures represent diopters."

"And an adjustment of negative five certainly blurs the entire—"

"That can't be an adjustment," the major interposed. "Someone has idly turned that eyepiece."

"I see your point," Mason said and promptly turned the eyepiece back to zero. "There," he announced, "that's better."

It was now possible to make out details in what had before been merely a patch of shadow.

Mason swung the binoculars to the picnic ground and could see quite plainly the masonry barbecue pits, the tables and chairs. Beyond them, through the trees he caught a glimpse of the ocean.

"A beach down there?" he asked.

"Not a beach, but a very fine place for surf fishing."

Mason swung the binoculars once more toward the clump of trees and the wide place in the road. "And you say people picnic there?"

"Occasionally, yes."

"From that point," Mason said, "one could see the house quite plainly with binoculars."

"But the binoculars are up here."

"Not the only pair in the world surely."

The major frowned. Mason turned the glasses on a moving object and saw a magnified image of Paul Drake walking slowly along a bridle path. The short, somewhat cramped steps indicated that his brief experience in the English riding saddle had been more than ample. The detective was leading the horse, his head bowed as he plodded along the bridle path.

CHAPTER THREE

MASON WAITED until he saw Major Winnett leave the house, walking toward the stables. Then the lawyer quietly opened the door of his room, walked down the corridor to Winnett's bedroom, crossed the balcony and climbed to the rail.

The entrance to the swallow's nest was too small to accommodate the lawyer's hand, but he enlarged it by clipping away bits of the dried mud with his thumb and forefinger.

From inside the nest came faint rustlings of motion. An immature beak pushed against Mason's finger.

The parent swallows cried protests as they swooped in swift, stabbing circles around the lawyer's head, but Mason, working rapidly, enlarged the opening so he could insert his hand into the nest. He felt soft down-covered bodies. Down below them, his groping fingers encountered only the concave surface of the nest.

A frown of annoyance crossed the lawyer's face. He continued groping, however, gently moving the young birds to one side. Then the frown faded as the tips of his fingers struck a hard metallic object.

As the lawyer managed to remove this object, sunlight scintillated an emerald and diamond brooch into brilliance.

Mason swiftly pocketed the bit of jewelry and drew back from the fierce rushes of the swallows. He dropped to the floor of the balcony and returned to the bedroom.

Back in the bedroom, he made a swift, thorough search of the various places where small objects might be concealed. A sole leather gun case in the back of a closet contained an expensive shotgun. Mason looked through the barrels. Both were plugged with oiled rags at breech and muzzle.

Mason's knife extracted one of the rags. He tilted up the barrels, and jewelry cascaded out into his palm, rings, earrings, brooches, a diamond and emerald necklace.

Mason replaced the jewelry, inserted the rag once more and put the gun back in the leather case, then returned the case to the closet.

Preparing to leave the room, he listened for a few moments at the bedroom door, then boldly opened it and stepped out, retracing his steps toward his own room.

He was halfway down the corridor when Mrs. Victoria Winnett appeared at an intersecting corridor and moved toward Mason with stately dignity and a calm purpose.

"Were you looking for something, Mr. Mason?" she asked.

The lawyer's smile was disarming. "Just getting acquainted with the house."

Victoria Winnett was the conventional composite of a bygone era. There were pouches beneath her eyes, sagging lines to her face, but the painstakingly careful manner in which every strand of hair had been carefully coiffed, her face massaged, powdered, and rouged, indicated the emphasis she placed on appearance, and there was a stately dignity about her manner which, as Della Street subsequently remarked, reminded one of an ocean liner moving sedately up to its pier.

Had she carefully rehearsed her entrance and been grooming herself for hours to convey just the right impression of dignified rebuke, Mrs. Victoria Winnett would not have needed to change so much as a line of her appearance. "I think my *son* wanted to show you around," she said as she fell into step at Mason's side.

"Oh, he's done that already," Mason said with breezy informality. "I was just looking the place over."

"You're Mr. *Perry* Mason, the lawyer, aren't you?"

"That's right."

"I had gathered from what I read about your cases that you specialize mostly in trial work."

"I do."

"*Murder* trials, do you not?"

"Oh, I handle lots of other cases. The murder cases get the most publicity."

"I see," she said in the tone of one who doesn't see at all.

"Nice place you have here," the lawyer went on. "I am very much interested in that observation cubicle on top of the house."

"It was my husband's idea. He liked to sit up there. Didn't I hear the swallows crying out there?"

"I thought *I* heard them too," Mason said.

She looked at him sharply. "We try to keep them from nesting here, but occasionally the gardener fails to see a nest until it is completed. Then we don't disturb the nest until after the young birds have hatched. They're noisy and talkative. You can hear them quite early in the mornings. I trust they won't disturb you. Are you a sound sleeper, Mr. Mason?"

They had paused at the head of the stairs. Mrs. Winnett apparently did not intend to go down, so Mason, standing poised on the upper stair tread, used strategy to terminate the interview.

"My friend, Drake, is looking over the horses, and if you'll pardon me I'll run down and join him."

He flashed her a smile and ran swiftly down the stairs, leaving her standing there, for the moment nonplussed at the manner in which the lawyer had so abruptly forestalled further questions.

CHAPTER FOUR

IN THE PATIO, Della Street caught Perry Mason's eye, gave him a significant signal and moved casually over to the driveway where she climbed into the car and sat down.

Mason walked over. "I think Paul Drake has something," he said. "I'm going down and look him up. He's just coming in on the bridle path. What have you got?"

"I can tell you something about the nurse, chief."

"What?"

"In the first place, if a woman's intuition counts for anything, she's in love with the major—one of those hopeless affairs where she worships him from a distance. In the second place, I think she has a gambling habit of some sort."

"Races?"

"I don't know. I was up in the cupola just after you were. There was a pad of paper in the drawer of the little table up there. At first it looked completely blank. Then I tilted it so the light struck it at an angle and I could see that someone had written on the top sheet with a fairly hard pencil so it had made an imprint on the sheet under it. Then the top sheet had been torn off."

"Good girl! What was on the sheet of paper? I take it something significant."

"Evidently some gambling figures. I won't bother to show

you the original at this time, but here's a copy that I worked out. It reads like this: *These numbers* on the first line, then down below that, *led*; then down below that a space and 5"5936; down below that 6"8102; down below that 7"9835; down below that 8"5280; down below that 9"2640; down below that 10"1320."

"Anything else?" Mason asked.

"Then a line and below the line, the figure 49"37817. That looks like some sort of a lottery to me. I learned Mrs. Winnett has been up in the cupola lately, and since *she'd* hardly be a gambler, I assume the nurse must have written down the figures."

Mason said thoughtfully, "Notice the last three numbers, Della, 5280, 2640, 1320. Does that sequence mean something to you?"

"No, why?"

Mason said, "5280 feet in a mile."

"Oh, yes, I get that."

"The next number, 2640 feet is a half mile, and the last number, 1320 feet, is a quarter mile."

"Oh, yes, I see now. Then that double mark means inches, doesn't it?"

"It's an abbreviation of inches, yes. What does this nurse seem like, Della? Remember I only barely met her."

"Despite her muddy complexion, straight hair and glasses, her eyes are really beautiful. You should see them light up when the major's name comes up. My own opinion is this nurse could be good-looking. Then Mrs. Winnett would fire her. So she keeps herself looking plain and unattractive so she can be near the major, whom she loves with a hopeless, helpless, unrequited passion."

"Look here," Mason said, "if you've noticed that within an hour and a half, how about Mrs. Victoria Winnett? Doesn't she know?"

"I think she does."

"And hasn't fired the nurse?"

"No. I think she doesn't mind if the nurse worships the ground the major walks on but doesn't presume to raise her eyes to look at him, if you get what I mean."

"I get it," Mason said thoughtfully, "and I don't like it. Wait, here comes Paul now."

Drake, walking stiffly, joined them.

"Find anything, Paul?" Mason asked.

"I found something," Drake conceded, "and I don't know what it is."

"What does it look like, Paul?"

"In the first place," Drake said, "you can easily follow her tracks. She took the lower bridle path. After the first quarter mile, there's only one set of tracks going and coming. They were made when the ground was soft and they go down to a road and a gate that's locked. I didn't have a key, but I could see where the horse tracks went through the gate and down onto the road, so I tied up my horse and managed to squeeze through the fence."

"Any tracks around those trees, Paul?"

"An automobile had been parked there," Drake said. "There must have been two automobiles. That's the only way I can figure it out, but I still can't figure the tracks right."

"How come?"

Drake took a small thin book from his pocket. "This is a little pocketbook which gives the tread designs of all makes of tires. Now an automobile that had some fairly new tires was in there. One of the wheels was worn too much to identify, but I identified the track of a right front wheel. Then the track of the other front wheel and the other hind wheel and . . . well, there I bogged down, Perry."

"What do you mean?"

"Of course, you have to understand it's a little difficult

trying to get those tracks all fitted into the proper sequence.
They . . ."

"What are you getting at?" Mason said.

"Hang it, Perry, I got *three* wheels."

"And the fourth was worn smooth?"

"Not that—what I mean is, Perry, that I got three wheels
on a single side."

Mason frowned at the detective. "*Three* wheels on a side?"

"Three wheels on a side," Paul Drake insisted doggedly.

Mason said rather excitedly, "Paul, did you notice a cir-
cular spot in the ground, perhaps eight or ten inches in dia-
meter?"

"How the deuce did you know that spot was there?"
Drake demanded, his face showing bewilderment.

Mason said, "It was made by the bottom part of a bucket,
Paul. And the three tracks on each side were all right. That's
the way it should be."

"I don't get it."

"A house trailer," Mason explained. "An automobile and
a house trailer were parked under the trees. The waste water from a trailer sink is carried out through a drain to the
outside. A bucket is placed there to catch the water as it runs
off."

"That's it, all right," Drake admitted, then added mo-
rosely, "I'm kicking myself for not thinking of it, Perry."

Mason said, "It now begins to look as though Marcia Winnett had kept an appointment on Monday with someone in
a house trailer. And that seems to have been very much a
turning point in her life."

Drake nodded. "On Monday—that's a cold trail, Perry."

"It's the only one we have," Mason pointed out.

CHAPTER FIVE

MASON, STUDYING the tire tracks, said, "It was an automobile and a house trailer, Paul. The round place which marks the location of the spout bucket can be taken as being approximately in the middle of the trailer. You can see over here the mark of an auxiliary wheel attached to the front of the trailer to carry part of the weight while the trailer was parked. That enables us to estimate the length of the trailer."

Drake said, "The trailer must have been backed in between these trees, Perry."

Mason started prowling along the edge of the fence. "Took some clever handling to get it in there. Let's look around for garbage. If the trailer remained here overnight, there are probably some tin cans . . . . potato peelings, stuff of that sort."

Mason, Della Street and Drake separated, covering the ground carefully.

Abruptly Della said, "Chief, don't look too suddenly, but casually take a look up there at the big house on the hill. I think I saw someone moving in the glassed-in observation tower."

"I rather expected as much," Mason said, without even looking up. "However, it's something we can't help."

Drake exclaimed, "Here it is, Perry, a collection of tin cans and garbage."

Mason moved over to where Drake was standing. Here the water from the winter rains, rushing down the ditch at the side of the road, had eddied around one of the roots of the big live oak and formed a cave which extended some three feet back under the roots of the tree.

Mason, squatting on his heels, used two dry sticks to rake out the articles.

There were three cans which had been flattened under pressure, some peelings from onions and potatoes, waxed paper which had been wrapped around a loaf of bread, an empty glass container bearing a syrup label, and a crumpled paper bag.

Mason carefully segregated the items with his sticks. As he did so he kept up a running fire of conversation.

"That flattening of the cans is the trick of an old out-doorsman," he said.

"Why flatten them?" Della inquired.

"Animals get their heads stuck in cans sometimes," Mason said. "Moreover, cans take up less room when they're flattened and require a smaller hole when they're buried. This little garbage pit tells quite a story. The occupant of the trailer must have been a man. Notice the canned beans, a can of chili con carne, potatoes, bread, onions—no tomato peelings, no lettuce leaves, no carrots, in fact, no fresh vegetables at all. A woman would have had a more balanced diet. These are the smallest cans obtainable and . . . hello, what's this?"

Mason had pulled apart the paper bag as he talked. Now he brought out a small oblong slip of paper on which figures had been stamped in purple ink.

Della Street said, "That's a cash register receipt from one of the cash-and-carry grocery stores."

Mason picked up the receipt. "And a very interesting one," he said. "The man bought fifteen dollars and ninety-four cents' worth of merchandise. There's a date on the back of the slip and this other figure refers to the time. The groceries were bought at five minutes past eight on Saturday morning. It begins to look, Paul, as though this is where you take over."

"What do you want me to do?" Drake asked.

Mason said, "Get a room in the hotel at Silver Strand beach. Open up something of an office there. Get men on the job. Get lots of men. Have your men buy groceries. See if the printing on the slip from any cash register matches this. If it does, try to find out something about the single, sun-bronzed man who purchased fifteen dollars and ninety-four cents' worth of groceries at five minutes past eight on Saturday morning. A sale of that size to a man just a few minutes after the store opened might possibly have attracted attention."

"Okay," Drake said. "Anything else?"

"Lots else," Mason said. "Della, where's that slip of paper, the copy you made of what you found in the observation tower?"

Della ran to the glove compartment and brought back the square of paper on which she'd made the copy.

Drake looked at it, then said, "What is it, Perry?"

"Stuff Della found in the observation tower. What do you make of it?"

"Some sort of dimensions," Drake said. "Here's this number 8 inches and 5280 feet, 9 inches and half a mile, 10 inches and quarter of a mile. What's the idea, Perry? Why should the inches run 5, 6, 7, 8, 9, 10, and . . . ?"

"Suppose they aren't inches?" Mason said. "Suppose they're ditto marks."

"Well, it could be."

"Then what?" Mason asked.

Drake said, "Then the numbers could have something to do with a lottery of some sort."

"Add them up," Mason said dryly.

"The total is already here," Drake said. "49″37817."

Mason handed him a pencil.

Della Street, leaning over Drake's shoulder, was the first to get it. "Chief," she exclaimed, "the total isn't correct."

"I knew it wasn't," Mason said. "I didn't know just how much it was off, however. Let's find out."

Della Street said, "The total is . . . Wait a minute, Paul, I'll get it . . . 45″33113, but the total that's *marked* there is 49″37817."

"Subtract them," Mason said. "What do you get?"

Della Street's skillful fingers guided the pencil as she hastily wrote down numbers and performed the subtraction. "4″4704," she said.

Mason nodded. "I think," he said, "when we get this case solved, we'll find the important figure is the one that *isn't* there. Bear that figure in mind, Paul. It may turn up later."

CHAPTER SIX

PERRY MASON TOOK the steep stairs to the observation tower two at a time.

There was no one in the cupola. The binoculars, however, had once more been swung so that they were pointing to the grove of trees where the trailer had been parked. Mason placed his eyes to the binoculars. The left eye showed a clear vision, the right was blurred.

Mason bent over to study the adjustment on the right lens, saw it was set once more at negative five, then he changed the focus on the binoculars.

As he did so, he heard motion behind him and straightened abruptly.

Mrs. Victoria Winnett was standing in the doorway. At her side was a slender brunette in riding clothes whose face showed startled surprise. Mrs. Winnett's face showed no expression whatever.

"I hardly expected to find *you* here," Mrs. Winnett said to Mason and then, turning to the young woman at her side, said, "Miss Rexford, permit me to present Mr. Perry Mason, the lawyer."

Daphne Rexford favored Mason with a smile which went only as far as her lips. Her eyes showed an emotion which might have been merely nervousness, might have been panic.

Mason acknowledged the introduction, then said, "I'm fascinated with the view you get from here, Mrs. Winnett."

"My late husband spent much of his time here. The place does hold something of a fascination. Daphne loves it."

"You're here frequently?" Mason asked Daphne Rexford.

"Yes, I study birds."

"I see."

"But," she went on hastily, "since you're here, I'll postpone my bird study until some other time."

"On the contrary," Mason said, "I was just leaving. I wanted to get the lay of the land."

"He's working with Claude on a mining deal," Mrs. Winnett hastened to explain to Daphne Rexford. "There's a mining engineer with him. And Mr. Mason has his secretary. You'll meet them if you're over for dinner tonight."

"Oh, thank you, but I . . . I don't think I can make it for dinner tonight. If Claude's going to be busy . . . Where's Marcia?"

"Visiting friends," Mrs. Winnett said dryly. "*Please* come."

"Well, I . . . I should . . ."

Mason said as she hesitated, "Well, I must get down and hunt up my client. After all, I must earn my fee, you know."

"I feel quite sure you will," Mrs. Winnett said with a certain subtle significance. "Come, Daphne, dear. Draw up a chair. What was it you were saying about swallows?"

Daphne said hurriedly, "Oh, there's a meadowlark! I think there must be a nest down by that bush. I've seen that same lark so many times in that exact position. . . ."

Mason quietly closed the door and walked down the stairs.

Major Winnett was in the drawing room. He looked up as Mason crossed toward the patio. "What luck?" he asked.

"Progress," Mason said.

Major Winnett's lips tightened. "Can't you do better than

that? Can't you give me something definite? Or are you just running around in circles?"

"A good hound always runs around in circles to pick up a scent."

"Then you haven't anything definite yet?"

"I didn't say that."

"You intimated it."

Mason slid his right hand down into his trousers pocket and abruptly withdrew the diamond and emerald brooch he had taken from the swallow's nest.

"Seen this before?" he asked, extending his hand.

Major Winnett stiffened for a moment to rigid immobility. "It looks . . . Mr. Mason, that certainly is similar to a brooch my wife had."

"One that was stolen?"

"I believe so, yes."

"Thank you," Mason said and slipped the brooch back into his pocket.

"May I ask where you got that?" Claude Winnett asked excitedly.

"Not yet," Mason told him.

The telephone rang sharply. Major Winnett moved over to the library extension, picked up the receiver, said "Hello," then turned to Mason. "It's for you."

Mason took the telephone. Drake's voice said, "We've got something, Perry."

"What?"

"That oblong slip of paper from the cash register. We've located the store. The girl that was on duty remembers our party. We've got a good description now. With that to go on, we had no trouble picking up his trail in a trailer camp. He registered under the name of Harry Drummond."

"There now?" Mason asked.

"Not now. He pulled out early yesterday morning. I've got men covering every trailer camp anywhere near here. We should pick him up soon. We have the license number and everything. And here's a funny one, Perry. There's a jane looking for him."

"You mean . . . ?"

"No, not the one we're interested in, another one. She's brunette, snaky, young and tall, and she was asking the cashier about him earlier in the day. Had a good description. Wanted to know if such a man had been in."

"Are you located there in the hotel?"

"Yes. I've fixed up an office here and have half a dozen men out on the job, with more coming in all the time."

Mason said, "I'll be right up."

"Okay, be looking for you. Good-by."

Mason heard the click at the other end of the line but did not immediately hang up. He stood holding the receiver, frowning at the carpet.

Abruptly he heard another sharp click and the telephone bell in the library extension gave a little tinkle.

Mason dropped the receiver into place and turned to Major Winnett. "I take it," he said, "you have several extensions on the phone?"

"Four," Major Winnett said. "No, there's five. There's one up in the observation tower. I almost forgot about that."

"Thank you," Mason said, and then added after a moment, "so did I."

CHAPTER SEVEN

Paul Drake was talking on the phone as Mason entered the suite of rooms Drake was using for headquarters. In an adjoining room Della Street, a list of numbers at her elbow, was putting through a steady succession of calls.

"Come in, Perry," Drake said, hanging up the receiver. "I was trying to get you. We're getting results fast."

"Shoot."

"Our party is a man thirty-eight years old, bronzed, wears cowboy boots, a five-gallon hat, leather jacket, Pendleton trousers, rather chunky and has a wide, firm mouth. The license number of his automobile is 4E4705. He's driving a Buick and has quite an elaborate house trailer painted green on the outside with aluminum paint on the roof. Up until Saturday morning he was in the Silver Strand Trailer Camp. He left Saturday, showed up again late Monday night, pulled out again Wednesday morning and hasn't been seen since."

"How did you get it?" Mason asked.

"Just a lot of legwork."

"Give me the highlights."

"We located the store that has that cash register—the only one in town. Cash register gives the time and date of sale, the

amount of the items and the total. This sale was made shortly
after the store opened Saturday morning, and the cashier remembers the man's general appearance. She particularly remembered the cowboy boots. We started covering trailer
camps and almost immediately picked up our trail."

"What are you doing now?"

"I've got operatives scattered around with automobiles
covering every trailer camp, every possible parking place for
a house trailer anywhere in this part of the country. We're
working in a constantly widening circle and should turn up
something soon."

Mason took out his notebook. "The number is 4E4705?"

"That's right."

"Then our mysterious observer in the observation tower
made a mistake in addition. Remember, we were looking for
a number 4"4704. The first number must have been 4E4705
and ditto marks were beneath the E. The real total then
should have been . . ."

He was interrupted by a knock on the door, a quick stac-
cato knock which somehow contained a hint of hysteria.

Mason exchanged glances with Drake. The detective left
the desk, crossed over and opened the door.

The woman who stood on the threshold was twenty-seven
or twenty-eight, a tall brunette with flashing black eyes, high
cheekbones and an active, slender figure. A red brimless hat
perched well back on her head emphasized the glossy darkness of her hair and harmonized with the red of her carefully
made-up lips.

She smiled at Paul Drake, a stage smile which showed even,
white teeth. "Are *you* Mr. Drake?" she asked, glancing from
him to Mason.

Drake nodded.

"May I come in?"

Drake wordlessly stood to one side.

His visitor entered the room, nodded to Perry Mason and said, "I'm *Mrs.* Drummond."

Drake started to glance at Mason, then caught himself in time and managed to put only casual interest in his voice. "I'm Mr. Drake," he said, "and this is Mr. Mason. Is there something in particular, Mrs. Drummond?"

She said, "You're looking for my husband."

Drake merely raised his eyebrows.

"At the Silver Strand Trailer Camp," she went on nervously. "And *I'm* looking for him *too.* I wonder if we can't sort of pool information?"

Mason interposed suavely. "*Your* husband, and you're looking for him, Mrs. Drummond?"

"Yes," she said, her large dark eyes appraising the lawyer.

"How long since you've seen him?" Mason asked.

"Two months."

"Perhaps if you want us to *pool* information, you'd better tell us a little more about the circumstances and how you happened to know we were looking for him."

She said, "I'd been at the Silver Strand Trailer Camp earlier in the day. The man promised me that he'd let me know if my husband returned. When your detectives appeared and started asking questions, he took the license number of their car, found out it belonged to the Drake Detective Agency and . . ." She laughed nervously and said, "And that is where I started to do a little detective work on my own. Are you looking for him for the same reason I am?"

Mason smiled gravely. "That brings up the question of why you're looking for him."

She gave an indignant toss of her head. "After all, I have nothing to conceal. We were married a little over a year ago. It didn't click. Harry is an outdoors man. He's always chasing

around on the trail of some mining deal or some cattle ranch.
I don't like that sort of life and . . . well, about two months
ago we separated. I sued for divorce."

"Have you got it yet?"

"Not yet. We had an understanding about a property settlement. When my lawyer sent my husband the papers, he
sent them back with an insulting note and said he wouldn't
pay me a red cent and that if I tried to get tough about it,
he'd show that I didn't have any rights whatever."

"Why?"

"I don't know."

"And you want to find out just what he means by that?"
Mason asked.

"That's right. And now suppose you tell me what *you* want
him for. Has he done something?"

"Is he the type who would?" Mason asked.

"He's been in trouble before."

"What sort of trouble?"

"A mining swindle."

Drake glanced inquiringly at Mason.

"Where are you located?" Mason asked Mrs. Drummond.

"I'm right here at the hotel. And don't think they're the
ones who told me about Mr. Drake's being here," she added
hastily. "I found that out by . . . in another way."

"You spoke of *pooling* information," Mason said sug-
gestively.

She laughed and said, "Well, what I meant was if you find
him, will you let me know? And if I find him, I could let you
know. After all, he shouldn't be difficult to locate with that
trailer, but I want to catch him before he can get out of the
state. If I can find out where he is, I have—some papers to
serve."

"You have a car?" Mason asked.

She nodded, then added by way of explanation, "That is

one thing I salvaged out of our marriage. I made him buy
me a car, and that's one of the reasons I want to see him. The
car's still in his name. He agreed to let me have it as part
of the property settlement, but in his letter to my lawyer he
said he could even take the car away from me if I tried to
make trouble. Does either of you gentlemen have any idea
what he meant by that?"

Mason shook his head and Drake joined in the gesture of
negation.

"Perhaps," Mason suggested, "we might work out something. You see, even if your assumption is correct that we
are looking for your husband, we would be representing some
client in the matter and would naturally have to discuss
things with that client."

"Is it because of something he's done?" she asked appre-
hensively. "Is he in more trouble? Will it mean all his money
will go for lawyers again, just like it did before?"

"I'm sure I couldn't tell you," Mason said.

"That means you won't. Look, I'm in room six-thirteen.
Why don't you ask your *client* to come and see me?"

"Will you be there all during the evening?" Drake asked.

"Well . . ." She hesitated. "I'll be in and out. I'll . . . I'll
tell you what I'll do. I'll keep in touch with the hotel and if
there are any messages, I'll be where I can come and get
them."

She flashed them a smile, moved toward the door with
quick, lithe grace, then almost as an afterthought turned
and gave them her hand, glancing curiously through the
open door of the adjoining room to where Della Street was
seated at the telephone. Then she gave Mason another smile
as the lawyer held the door open for her, and left the room,
walking with quick nervous steps.

Mason closed the door and cocked a quizzical eyebrow at
Paul Drake.

"The guy's wise," Drake said. "That means we haven't much time, Perry."

"You think he was watching his back trail?"

Drake nodded. "She's an alert little moll who knows her way around. This man Drummond has done something that he's trying to cover up. He left her to watch his back trail. She hypnotized the man who runs the trailer camp and then when my man showed up in an agency car—"

"But how about her asking questions at the cash-and-carry, Paul?"

Drake snapped his fingers. "Shucks, there's nothing to *that*. That's the way she builds up a background for herself. After all, she—"

The telephone interrupted. Drake picked up the receiver, said, "Drake talking. . . . Okay, let's have it . . . When? . . . Where? . . . Okay, stay on the job. . . . We'll be right down."

Drake hung up the receiver, saying, "Well, that's it. We've got him located."

"Where?"

"Little down-at-the-heel trailer camp in a eucalyptus grove about three miles from here. Not much of a place, auto-court cabins in front and, as an afterthought because there was lots of room, the owner strung up some wires and advertised trailer space in the rear. The conveniences aren't too good and it's patronized mostly by people who want to save two bits a day on the regular parking rate. The chief advantage is lots of elbowroom. The grove consists of several acres, and if a man wants to walk far enough to the bath and shower, he can pick his own parking place for the trailer."

"Any details?" Mason asked.

"One of my men just located it. The trailer came in yesterday night. The man who runs the place was busy selling gasoline at the time, and the driver of the car called out that he'd come back and register later. He tossed the man a silver dollar and the man told him to park any place he wanted to where he could find a plug for his electric connection."

Mason said, "Let's go. Della, you stay here and run the place. We'll telephone you in half an hour or so."

They drove down to the trailer camp in Mason's car. Drake's operative, lounging casually in the door of one of the auto cabins, gave the detective a surreptitious signal and pointed toward the adjoining cabin.

Registering simply as "P. Drake," the detective rented the vacant cabin, then settled down with Perry Mason. A few moments later Drake's operative came across to join them.

"Ever met Pete Brady?" Drake asked Mason.

Mason shook hands, saying, "I've seen him once or twice before around your office."

"Glad to know you," Brady said to Mason, and then to Drake, "I'm not certain but what the guy who runs the place is getting a little suspicious. I asked too many questions."

"What's the dope?"

"The trailer's out there attached to the car. So far, I haven't had a glimpse of the man who is in it, but it's the license number of the car we want okay—4E4705."

"Let's take a look around," Mason said.

"You'll have to take it easy," Brady warned. "Just sort of saunter around."

"How about the gag of buying a trailer?" Drake asked. "Have you used that?"

Brady shook his head.

"We'll try that," Drake said. "You can wait here for a while. What's the guy's name who runs the place?"

"Elmo, Sidney Elmo."

"Did he see you come over here?"

"No. I waited until he was selling gas."

"Okay. Stick around. I'll go tell the bird that we heard one of the trailers here was for sale. He won't know anything about it. That gives us an opportunity to go sauntering around looking them over."

Five minutes later when Drake returned, Mason joined him and they walked slowly out past the line of somewhat dilapidated cabins into the eucalyptus grove. Late afternoon shadows made the place seem cold and gloomy. The ground was still moist from the rain and the drippings of the trees when ocean fog enveloped that portion of the country.

"There's the outfit," Drake said. "What do we do? Go right up and knock and ask him if it's for sale?"

Mason said, "Let's try one of the other trailers first. We can talk loud enough so our voices will carry over here."

"Good idea," Drake said.

"Take this one," Mason suggested.

The two walked over to the small homemade trailer Mason had indicated. It was parked about a hundred feet from the green trailer. Electric lights showed a well-fleshed woman in her late forties cooking over the stove. On the outside, a man was taking advantage of the failing light to tinker with the bumper on the trailer. There was an Oklahoma license plate on the car.

"This the outfit that's for sale?" Mason asked.

The man looked up, a long, thin mouth twisted into a smile. He said with a drawl, "I ain't saying yes, and I ain't saying no. You want to buy?"

"We're looking for a trailer that we heard was for sale here."

"What sort of a trailer?"

"We just heard it was a good one."

"That's the description of this job all right."

Drake interposed, "You're not the man who spoke to the

manager of the Silver Strand Trailer Camp and said he
wanted to sell, are you?"

"Nope. Fact is, I'm not particularly anxious to sell. But
if you wanted to buy it, I'd be willing to listen."

"We're looking for a particular trailer that's for sale,"
Mason explained. "How about that green one over there?
Know anything about it?"

"No. It just came in last night."

"Don't suppose you've talked with the people who own
it?"

"I ain't seen 'em. They haven't been around all day."

Mason said, "That looks like it. Let's go over there, Paul."

"Take it easy," Mason said as they approached. "Ever use
a house trailer, Paul?"

"No. Why?"

"The steady weight of the trailer has a tendency to wear
out springs. So most trailers are equipped with an auxiliary
wheel which can be screwed into position when the trailer is
parked."

"There isn't any here," Drake said.

"That's just the point. Furthermore, no spout bucket has
been put out under the spout. And to cap the climax, the
cord hasn't been connected with the electric outlet."

"What are you getting at, Perry?"

By way of reply, Mason knocked loudly on the trailer door.
When there was no response, the lawyer tentatively tried the
knob.

The door swung open.

There was still enough afternoon light to show the sprawled
figure lying on the floor. The dark pool eddying out from
under the body showed little jagged streaks of irregularity,
but its ominous significance could not be misjudged.

"Oh-oh!" Drake exclaimed.

Mason stepped up and entered the trailer. Carefully avoid-

ing the red pool, he looked down at the body. Then he bent
over, touched the high-heeled cowboy boot, moved it gently
back and forth.

"Been dead for some time, Paul. Rigor mortis has set in."

"Come on out," Drake begged. "Let's play this one on the
up-and-up and notify the police."

"Just a minute," Mason said. "I . . ." He bent over, and
as he did so a shaft of light struck his face.

"What's that?" Drake asked.

Mason moved slightly so that the beam of light struck his
eyes.

"That," he announced, "is a hole in this trailer, directly in
line with the window of that Oklahoma trailer. Light from
the window over there where the woman is cooking comes
through the hole in this trailer. The hole could have been
made by a bullet."

"Okay, Perry. Let's notify the police."

Mason said, "First I want to find out a little more about
that Oklahoma trailer."

"For the luvva Mike, Perry, have a heart! You're in the
clear on this one—so far."

Mason, moving cautiously, left the trailer. He hesitated a
moment when he stepped to the ground. Then he carefully
polished the doorknob with his handkerchief.

"That's removing evidence," Drake said. "There are
other prints there besides yours."

"How do you know?"

"It stands to reason."

"You can't prove it," Mason said. "The murderer probably wiped his fingerprints off the door just as I did."

Mason walked back to the trailer with the Oklahoma license. The man, still bent over the bumper at the rear of
the trailer, seemed to be working aimlessly, stalling for time.

The position of his head indicated an interest in what had been going on over at the other trailer.

"That the one?" he asked as Mason approached.

"I don't know. No one seems to be home."

"I ain't seen 'em leave. They couldn't go very far without their car."

"Seen any visitors over there?" Mason asked casually.

"Not today. There was a young woman called last night."

"What time?"

"I don't know. We'd gone to bed. Her headlights shone in the window and woke me up when she came. I sat up in bed and looked out the window."

"See her plain?"

"Yeah—a redhead. Checkered suit—trim-looking package."

"She go in?"

"I guess so. She switched off her lights and I went back to sleep. Woke me up again when she left. Her car backfired a couple of times."

Mason glanced at Drake. "I'd like to find these people."

"I think there's only one—a man. He drove in last night and had quite a bit of trouble backing the trailer around. You take one of these big trailers and it's quite a job to park it. You try to back up and everything's just reversed from what it is when you're backing just a car. We went to bed pretty early and sometime after I'd got to sleep this other car came up. What really woke me up was headlights shining in my window. I looked out and seen this woman."

"Remember what sort of car she was driving?"

"It was a rented car."

"How do you know?"

"From the gasoline rationing stamp on the windshield."

"Your wife didn't wake up?"

"No."

"How long have *you* been here?" Mason asked.

"What's it to you?"

"Nothing."

"I thought not," the man said, suddenly suspicious, and then after a moment added, "You're asking a lot of questions."

"Sorry," Mason said.

The man hesitated a moment, then, by way of dismissal, turned back to the bumper.

Mason glanced significantly at Paul Drake. Silently the two walked away.

"Okay, Paul," Mason said in a low voice. "Get Della on the phone. Tell her to put operatives on every drive-yourself car agency within a radius of fifty miles and see if we can find where the woman rented the car. When we spot the place, I'll handle the rest of it."

"I don't like it," Drake said.

"I don't like it myself," Mason told him. "But the young woman who called there last night was Marcia Winnett."

"And her car backfired," Drake said dryly.

Mason met his eyes. "Her car backfired, Paul. And in case it ever becomes necessary, remember that the only person who heard it said it was a backfire."

Drake nodded gloomily. "Not that *that* will do any good, Perry."

"It keeps us in the clear, Paul. You don't rush to the police to report that someone's car backfired."

"When you've discovered a body, you do."

"Who knows we've discovered any body?"

"I do."

Mason laughed. "Back to the hotel, Paul. Try to trace that car. And just to be on the safe side, find out where Mrs. Drummond was last night."

CHAPTER EIGHT

THE LAST TASK Mason had given Paul Drake turned out to be simple. Mrs. Drummond had been trying to locate her husband in the nearby trailer camps all the evening before, and she had arranged with a police officer who was off duty to accompany her.

Locating the rented car in which the girl in the checkered suit went to the trailer camp was another matter.

Despite all of Drake's efficiency, it was nearing eight o'clock when his detectives uncovered the lead Mason wanted. A man who operated a car rental agency in one of the coast cities, some twenty-five miles from Silver Strand Beach, had rented a car to a young woman who wore a checkered suit and who answered the description of Marcia Winnett.

Drake looked up from the telephone. "Want my man to try to pick up the trail from there or do you want to do it, Perry?"

Mason said, "I'll do it, Paul. And it might be best to let your man think that that isn't the trail we want."

"Okay," Drake said, and then into the telephone, "Describe her, Sam. Uh-huh . . . uh-huh, well, that's not the one. Keep working. Cover those other agencies and then report."

Drake hung up the phone. "Want me to come along, Perry?"

"Della and I'll handle it," Mason said. "Start calling your

men in. Let them feel it turned out to be a false lead. And
you'd better start checking on Mrs. Drummond, Paul. I
wouldn't like to have her show up right now."

Drake nodded and said solicitously, "Watch your step,
Perry."

"I'm watching it. Come on, Della."

The man who operated the car rental agency which had
furnished a car to Marcia Winnett was not particularly com-
municative. It took diplomacy to get him in the mood to
talk. Even then he confined his information to bare essen-
tials.

He had never seen his customer before. She gave her name
as Edith Bascom. She said her mother had died and it was
necessary for her to use a car in connection with handling
the estate. She was registered at the local hotel.

"Do you check on these stories?" Mason asked. "Or do you
just rent cars?"

"Sometimes we just rent cars. Sometimes we check."

"What did you do in this case?"

"Cars are scarce now," the man said. "We checked."

"How?"

The man picked up a daily paper dated the day before
and indicated the obituary column. Mason followed the man's
finger to the stereotyped announcement of the death of Mrs.
Shirley Bascom and the statement that funeral arrangements
would be private.

Mason said, "I guess that covers it all right."

"What's your interest in it?"

"I'm a lawyer."

"I see. Well, she's okay. Rather upset on account of her
mother's death, but a nice girl. You'll find her in the Palace
Hotel, two blocks down the street."

"You checked on that?"

"I told you cars are scarce," the man said. "I checked on it."

It was but a matter of routine for Mason and his secretary to get the number of the room which had been assigned to Edith Bascom. Two minutes later Mason was knocking on the door.

There was no answer. Mason tried the knob. The door was locked.

Mason made a swift survey of the hall, stooped and held out his hands. "Step on my hands, Della. Take a quick look through the transom."

She braced herself with a hand on his shoulder, caught the lower ledge of the transom and peered through.

Mason, with his right hand on her hip, steadying her, felt her body stiffen. Then she was scrambling to get down.

"Chief," she said in an ominous whisper, "she's stretched out on the bed. She's . . . terribly still."

"Lights on?"

"No, but the shade is up and there's enough light coming in from the electric sign in front to make out the form on the bed."

Mason said, "There's a spring lock on the door. . . . Better take another look, Della. See if she's breathing and . . . hold it. Here comes a chambermaid."

The chambermaid who wearily approached was aroused only momentarily from the lethargy of overwork by the bill Mason pushed into her palm.

"My wife and I seem to have left our key downstairs. If you could let us in, it would save us a trip down . . ."

"It's against the rules," she said, then added tonelessly, "but I guess it's okay." Producing her passkey, she clicked back the latch on the door.

Mason boldly pushed open the door, stood aside for Della

to enter, then followed her into the dimly lighted room and closed the door behind him.

Della Street crossed over to the woman lying on the bed, as Mason groped for her pulse.

"She's alive!" Della Street said.

"The light," Mason said crisply. "Pull the curtains first."

Della Street jerked down the shades, ran over and switched on the light.

Mason glanced at the bottle of sleeping tablets by the side of the bed, picked up the newspaper on the floor and glanced at it.

"She must have taken them yesterday," Della said. "We'll need a doctor and—"

"This afternoon," Mason interrupted curtly. "This is a late edition of the afternoon paper."

He dropped the paper, shook the sleeper and said, "Towels, Della. Cold water."

Della Street grabbed towels and turned on the cold water in the bathroom. Mason slapped Marcia Winnett with cold towels until the eyelids flickered open.

"What is it?" she asked thickly.

Mason said to Della Street, "Run down to the drugstore, Della. Get an emetic. Have room service send up some black coffee."

"How about a doctor?"

"Not if we can avoid it. Let's hope she hasn't had the tablets down long enough to get the full effects. Get an emetic."

Marcia Winnett tried to say something, but the words were unintelligible. She dropped back against Mason's shoulder.

Mason calmly started removing her blouse. Della Street dashed from the room, headed for the drugstore.

Thirty minutes later Mason and Della Street assisted Marcia Winnett from the bathroom. There was a dead, lack-

luster look about her eyes, but she could talk now, and the
coffee was beginning to take effect.

Mason said, "Concentrate on what I'm telling you. I'm a
lawyer. I'm retained to represent you."

"By whom?"

"Your husband."

"No, no, he mustn't . . . he can't . . ."

Mason said, "I'm *your* lawyer. Your husband retained me
to help you. I don't have to tell him anything."

She sighed wearily and said, "Let me go. It's better this
way."

Mason shook her once more into wakefulness. "You went
riding Monday morning. You talked with a man in a trailer.
He made demands on you. You had to have money and have
it at once. You didn't dare to ask your husband for it."

Mason waited for an answer. She made none. Her eyelids
drooped and raised as if by a conscious effort.

Mason said, "You went back to the house. You canceled
the insurance on your jewelry because you were too conscientious to stick the insurance company. You arranged
to have some repairs made to a window on the side of your
bedroom so a ladder would be handy. You got up in the
night, went out to the balcony, and dumped your jewelry
into the swallow's nest. Then you started screaming."

Her face might have been a wooden mask.

Mason went on, "You had waited until Tuesday to stage
the burglary. You knew that it would be too obvious if it
happened Monday night, the day you had canceled the insurance. Wednesday morning you found an opportunity to
get most of the jewelry out of the swallow's nest. There was
one piece you overlooked. Now then, suppose you tell me
what happened after that."

She said, with the drowsy calm of one who discusses a distant event which can have no personal bearing, "I wanted to kill him. I can't remember whether I did or not."

"Did you shoot him?"

"I can't remember a thing that happened after . . . after I left the house."

Mason glanced at Della Street, said, "If I'm going to help you, I have to know what hold that man had on you."

"His name is Harry Drummond. He was my first husband."

"You were divorced?"

"I *thought* I was divorced. There were reasons why I couldn't go to Nevada. I gave him the money. He went to live in Nevada.

"From time to time he sent me reports of how things were coming. Twice he asked for more money. Then he wrote me the divorce had been granted. He was lying. He'd gambled the money away. There never had been a divorce."

"When did you find this out?" Mason asked.

"Monday morning," she said. "He was clever. He'd kept in touch with me. He knew I rode down along that bridle path. He parked his trailer there. Mrs. Victoria Winnett doesn't like to have people camp there, so I rode down to ask whoever was in the trailer to please move on down to the public campgrounds."

"You had no idea who was in the trailer?"

"Not until Harry opened the door and said, 'Hello, Marcia. I thought it was about time you were showing up.' "

"What did he want?"

"Money."

"And he threatened you with—what?"

"The one weapon Claude couldn't stand, notoriety."

"So you promised to get him money?"

"I promised to get him my jewelry. He had to have money at once. He said someone was putting screws on him for cash."

"You were to meet him there when?"

"Wednesday morning."

"So you manipulated this fake burglary on Tuesday night after canceling your insurance on Monday. Then you took him the jewelry. Did he ask you how you had managed to secure the jewelry?"

"Yes. I told him the whole story. I told him it was all right to pawn it because the Winnetts wouldn't report the burglary to the police."

"And then what happened?"

"I can't remember."

"What can't you remember?"

"I can't remember a thing from the time . . . from the time Harry took the jewelry. He made some sneering remark, and I remember becoming very angry and then . . . then my mind went entirely blank."

"Did you have a revolver with you when you went down to the trailer Wednesday morning?" Mason asked.

"Yes."

"Where did you get it?"

"From a bureau drawer."

"Whose gun was it?"

"I don't know. I think it was . . . Mrs. Winnett's gun— pearl-handled. I thought I might need some protection. It was a crazy idea. I took it along."

"Where is that gun now?"

"I don't know. I tell you I can't remember a thing that happened after I gave him the jewelry and he made that sneering remark."

"Did he make some further demands on you? Did he tell you you had to meet him at an isolated trailer park last night?"

"I don't know. I can't remember."

"*Did* you meet him there?"

"I can't remember."

"Did you," Mason asked, "rent an automobile from a drive-yourself agency about two blocks down the street?"

Her forehead puckered into a frown. "I seem to have some faint recollection of doing something like that, but I . . ." She shook her head. "No, it eludes me. I can't remember."

Mason said impatiently, "Why don't you come clean? You were clever enough to read the obituary notices and pretend to be the daughter of a woman who had just died. I'm trying to help you. At least tell me what I'm up against."

"I don't know. I can't remember."

Mason motioned toward the bottle of sleeping tablets. "And you thought you could take this way out and it would help?"

"I don't know. I guess I must have been . . . perhaps I was nervous. Perhaps I hadn't been sleeping at all and I just took too large a dose. I can't remember."

Mason turned to Della Street. "Willing to take a chance, Della?"

She nodded. "Anything you say, chief."

Mason said, "Put her in a car. Take her into Los Angeles. See that there's plenty of money in her purse. Take her to a *private* hospital. Under no circumstances give *your* name or address. Put on the rush act. Tell the first nurse you meet that this woman accosted you on the street and asked you to help her find out who she was. That you think it's a racket of some sort, but that she seems to have money, and if she needs any assistance, the hospital is the place where she should be able to get it. Then turn and get out of the door fast."

Della nodded.

Mason turned to Marcia Winnett. "You heard what I said?"

"Yes . . . I . . . you mustn't take chances for me. I know

that I must have killed him. I can't remember the details, Mr. Mason, but I killed him. I *think* it was in self-defense. I can't remember."

"I know," Mason said gently. "Don't worry about it. Remember you're a widow now. Don't get your memory back, and the next time you see me remember I'm a stranger. I'm going to try to help you. Get started, Della. Drive with the window open. Let her get lots of cold air. Get her to a hospital."

"How'll *you* get back?" Della asked.

"I'll have one of Drake's men pick me up."

Della looked at Marcia with cold contempt. "If you ask me," she blurted indignantly, "this act of hers . . ."

Mason gently closed one eye in an owlish wink. "Take her to the hospital, Della . . . and be sure you get out from under."

CHAPTER NINE

THE GRAVEL on the driveway caused the wheels to slide as Mason slammed on the brakes. The car skidded at a sharp angle and Mason didn't even bother to straighten it out. He snapped off the lights and the ignition, leaped out and headed up the steps of the Winnett mansion, pushed open the door, and strode into the drawing room unannounced.

Mrs. Victoria Winnett and Daphne Rexford were lingering over liqueurs, talking in low voices.

Mrs. Winnett's smile was distantly friendly. "*Really,* Mr. Mason," she said, "you're rather late—for dinner."

The lawyer merely nodded, glancing at Daphne Rexford.

Mrs. Winnett reached for the bell. "I presume I can get you something," she said. "But after this, if you don't mind—"

"Let the food go," Mason said. "I want to talk with you."

The finger which had been touching the bell remained motionless. She said, "*Really,* Mr. Mason," in a voice that indicated a polite rebuke.

Daphne Rexford hurriedly arose. "If you'll excuse me, I have a telephone call I want to make . . ."

"Sit down, my dear. After all, I can't permit this human tornado to come bursting in on our tête-à-tête with . . ."

64

Mason caught Daphne Rexford's eye and jerked his head. She made a feeble attempt at a smile and left the room.

"Really, Mr. Mason," Mrs. Winnett said, her voice now quite cold. "My attachment to my son is such that I am willing to make all allowances for his friends. Even so . . ."

She let her unfinished sentence carry its own meaning.

Mason drew up a chair and sat down. "Where's the major?"

"He was called out about twenty minutes ago."

"You're fond of Daphne Rexford, aren't you?"

"Of course."

"Was she in the observation tower Monday?"

"Really, Mr. Mason. I'm not on the witness stand."

"You're going to be," Mason said.

"I'm afraid you've been drinking."

"If you think this is a joke," Mason said, "just keep on stalling. Time is precious. The officers may be out here any minute."

"Officers?"

"Officers. Cops. Bulls. Detectives. Plain-clothes men. Newspaper photographers. Walking around here with their hats on, throwing cigarettes on the rugs, taking flashlight pictures with captions—'Society Leader Insists on Innocence.'"

That last did it. Mason saw her wince.

"You're a good poker player, but you can't bluff now. This is a showdown, Mrs. Winnett."

"Just what do you want?"

"To know all that you know."

She took a quick breath. "I know some trouble has developed between Marcia and Claude. I think that Marcia has left him. I hope she has."

"Why?"

"Because I don't feel that they are destined to be happy together . . ."

"No, I mean why has she left him?"

"I don't know."

"Make a guess."

"I can't."

"You know something about what happened on Monday?"

"On *Monday?* No."

"Was Daphne in the cupola on Monday?"

"I think she was."

"Did she come to you and tell you anything about what she saw either Monday or Wednesday?"

"Mr. Mason, you're being impertinent!"

Mason said, "You've found out something about Marcia. You thought she had involved the family good name, and took it on yourself to try to avoid notoriety. Your attempt backfired. I'm trying to find out just how badly it backfired."

"You can't prove any of these things you're saying, Mr. Mason."

"That," Mason said, "is only because I haven't the facilities at my command that the police have. The police may prove it."

"They won't," she said coldly. "I have told you absolutely everything I know."

Mason pushed back his chair, started for the door which led to the patio, then abruptly whirled, tiptoed swiftly back to the drawing room door, and jerked it open.

Daphne Rexford, plainly embarrassed, tried to pretend she had just been approaching the door. "Heavens," she said, laughing, "I thought we were going to have a collision, Mr. Mason. You seem in a hurry." She tried to push easily on past him.

Mason barred her way. "You were listening."

"Mr. Mason, how *dare* you say anything like that?"

"Come in," Mason said. "Let's have it out. Let's . . . no, on second thought, I think I'll talk with you alone. Come on."

Mason took her arm. She drew back.

Mrs. Winnett said, "Mr. Mason is completely overstepping the prerogatives of a guest. I dislike to ask him to leave in my son's absence, but . . ."

Mason said to Daphne Rexford, "Police are going to be swarming over the place before midnight. Do you want to talk to me or do you want to talk to them?"

Daphne Rexford said over her shoulder to Mrs. Winnett, "Good heavens, Victoria, let's humor the man! I'll be back within a few minutes."

Without waiting for an answer from Victoria Winnett, she smiled disarmingly at Mason and moved away from the drawing room. "Come on, where do you want to talk?"

"Over here's good enough," Mason said, stopping in a corner of the library.

Daphne Rexford stood facing him. "What," she asked in a low voice, "are the police going to be investigating?"

Mason met her eyes. "Murder."

"Who . . . who was killed?"

"Let's talk first about what *you* know," Mason said. "You're the one who has the trick right eye. Mrs. Winnett has been covering up for you."

"I'm afraid I don't know what you mean."

"Whenever you look through the binoculars," Mason explained, "you have to move the right eyepiece quite a distance in order to see clearly, don't you?"

"What if I do?"

Mason said, "*You* were the one who was watching Marcia on Monday. What did you see?"

"Nothing. I—"

"Were you here Monday? Were you in the observation cupola?"

"I believe I was."

"You're over here quite a bit?"

"Yes. Victoria and I are great friends. She's an older woman, of course, but I like her. I like what she stands for and—"

"And like to be near Major Winnett and see as much of him as you can?"

"Certainly not," she said indignantly.

"We'll let it go at that for the time being," Mason said. "Now, about Monday, what did you see?"

"Nothing. I—"

"You were up in the tower?"

"Yes. I go there quite frequently. I study birds, and I write poetry. I can get inspiration up there, and—"

"And keep an eye on Major Winnett's wife when she's around the grounds, I suppose?"

"Mr. Mason, that's unfair and untrue."

"All right. You saw her Monday. What did you see?"

"I . . . nothing."

Mason said, "You saw her go into that orange trailer that was parked down in the trees. You watched her—"

"It wasn't orange. It was green."

Mason grinned at her.

"All right," she said. "Don't think you're trapping me. I just happened to notice Marcia riding, and then I saw a house trailer parked in the trees."

"Did you see her go in?"

"I saw her tie up her horse and walk over toward the trailer. I wasn't interested. I returned to the poetry I was writing."

"How long was she in there?"

"I don't know."

"Why did you watch her?"

"I didn't watch her. I was looking at birds."

"You had a pencil and a pad of paper up there with you?"

"Yes, of course. I told you I write poetry. One doesn't write on the walls, Mr. Mason. I keep pencil and paper in the drawer of the table up there."

"You used the binoculars to get the license number of the automobile. You marked it down, didn't you?"

"No."

"When were you up there last writing poetry?"

"Why . . . why, today."

"Do you go up there every day?"

"Not every day, but quite frequently."

"Have you been up every day this week?"

"I . . . I guess I have. Yes."

The telephone rang, a sharp, strident, shrill summons.

Mason waited, listening, heard the butler answer it. Then the butler walked with unhurried dignity across the library to the drawing room and said something to Mrs. Winnett. She arose and went to the telephone. Mason heard her say, "Hello, Claude darling . . . Yes, dear . . . he's here. . . . I'm afraid, Claude, that there has been some misunderstanding. Mr. Mason's activities are hardly such as one would connect with a mining matter. He has shown quite an interest in what Marcia—"

Mason walked over, gently pushed her aside, took the receiver from her hand and said into the telephone, "Okay, Major, I've got it now. Get out here at once."

Major Winnett's voice was harsh with anger. "Just what do you mean, Mr. Mason? I'm afraid that you and I—"

Mason interrupted. "Your mother is trying to protect somebody. Daphne Rexford is trying to protect somebody. There's only one person I can think of whom they'd both go to such lengths to protect. That's you. If you get out here fast, we *may* be able to beat the police to it."

"What do you mean?"

"You know damn well what I mean," Mason said and hung up.

CHAPTER TEN

MAJOR WINNETT'S LIMP was more noticeable as he moved across the drawing room to confront Perry Mason. "I don't know exactly what's been going on here," he said angrily. "I don't know what prerogatives you have assumed, Mr. Mason. But as far as I'm concerned, our relationship is ended."

Mason said, "Sit down."

"I'm waiting to drive you to town, Mason, in case you don't have a car. If you do, I'll go with you to your room and you can pack up."

Mason said, "As nearly as I can put things together, you had previously discovered the trailer parked down in the trees. You were suspicious. You went up to the observation tower and saw Marcia go to the trailer and then later on saw the car and trailer go away. You took down the license number of the car. You looked up the man who owned that car. After that you kept a pretty close watch on what was going on.

"You didn't say anything when Marcia canceled the insurance on her jewelry and then had such an opportune burglary. You were very careful not to call the police because you knew the police would tab it as an inside job. You let your wife think it was because your mother didn't want any notoriety, but you got the jewelry and hid it in that twelve-gauge shotgun. After that you kept a pretty good watch on your wife. Where did you get the jewelry?"

"Mason," Winnett said coldly, "in case you don't leave this house at once, I'm going to call the servants and have you put out."

Mason brushed aside Major Winnett's angry statement with a gesture. "You'll have to hire more servants, then," he said, and went on. "When the trailer came back on Wednesday and Marcia went down there the second time, you decided to investigate. When you got down there, you found you had a fight on your hands. You killed Harry Drummond. Then you locked up the trailer, came back to the house and waited until dark. Then you took the trailer with its gruesome evidence of murder, drove to a trailer camp—"

"Mason, watch what you're saying. By heaven, I'll throw you out myself!"

"—parked the trailer," Mason went on, as smoothly as though Major Winnett had said nothing, "but only after some difficulty, then got out and went home. Then you felt it would add an artistic touch to have two shots fired so the *time* of the killing could be definitely fixed. So you went back, sneaked into the trailer park, stood in the dark *outside* the trailer and fired two shots in the air.

"You didn't realize that Marcia had been following you, and when she heard those shots she naturally thought you had killed Drummond out of jealousy, decided that she loved you too much to let you take the rap, and so skipped out. That's the reason you didn't go to a detective agency to get someone to try to find your wife. You wanted a lawyer who specialized in murder cases, *because you knew there was going to be a murder case.*"

Major Winnett snapped his fingers. "A lot of half-baked theories!"

"You see," Mason went on, "you made a couple of fatal

mistakes. One of them was that the first shot you fired missed Drummond and went clean through the trailer, leaving a hole in the double walls that clearly shows the direction taken by the bullet. When you parked that trailer in the automobile camp under the eucalyptus trees, it was dark and you didn't take the precaution of noticing where a bullet fired under such circumstances would have hit. That was a mistake, Major. As it happened, the hole in the trailer was lined up absolutely with the window of an adjoining trailer.

"At first the police will think the shot *might* have been fired from the other trailer. Then they'll make a more careful investigation and find that the direction of the bullet was the other way. Then they'll *know* that the murder wasn't committed there at the trailer park. There's another little thing you hadn't thought of. At the time you moved the trailer, the body had been dead for some time but the pool of blood hadn't entirely coagulated. Near the center of the pool there was blood that was still liquid. It spread around when the trailer swayed from side to side in going over irregularities in the road. That is what gives the pool of clotted blood the peculiar appearance of having little jagged streamers flowing from it."

Major Winnett was silent and motionless. His eyes were fixed on Mason with cold concentration. The anger had left his face, and it was quite plain the man's mind was desperately turning over Mason's words.

"So," Mason went on, "you knew that when the police started to investigate, they would find the dead man had been Marcia's first husband. You knew they would then start looking for her. When they found that she had skipped out, you knew what would happen. And so, you came to me."

Major Winnett cleared his throat. "You made a statement that Marcia had followed me. Do you have any evidence to back that up?"

Mason said, "It's a logical deduction from—"

"That's where you're wrong. Come to my room. I want to talk with you."

Mason said, "You haven't much time. The police have found the body. They're going to be out here looking for Marcia as soon as they have completed an identification and checked up on the man's history."

"All right," Winnett said, "come with me. Mother, you and Daphne pretend you haven't heard any of this. I'll talk with you later."

Major Winnett led the way to his room, opened a portable bar and took out a bottle of Scotch.

Mason refused with a gesture, then when Winnett had poured out a drink, the lawyer reached over and poured half of that drink back into the bottle. "Just enough to give yourself a bracer," he warned, "not enough to give you a letdown afterward. You're going to be talking with the police pretty soon. Start talking with me now."

Winnett said, "I didn't know Marcia went to visit the man in the trailer on Monday. I did know that Marcia went to the trailer on Wednesday."

"*How* did you know?"

"I was watching her."

"Why were you watching her?"

"Someone told me she had been to the trailer on Monday."

"Who?"

"My mother."

"What did you do?"

"After she left the trailer on Wednesday, I went down there to see who was in the trailer and see why my wife was having a rendezvous."

"What did you find?"

"I found the man dead. I found Marcia's jewelry spread

out on a table in front of him. I realized what must have happened. I saw that one shot had gone into the man's heart. One had apparently gone past his head and into the wall of the trailer."

"All right," Mason said sarcastically, "it's your story. Go ahead with it. What did you do then?"

"I took Marcia's jewelry and locked up the trailer. I came home. I waited until after dark, then I moved the trailer to a trailer camp I knew of, where I parked it. I got out and left the trailer and walked to where I had parked my own car earlier in the day. I had driven home before I realized that I could completely throw the police off the scent by letting it appear the murder had been committed late that night in the trailer camp. So I returned, stood near the trailer, fired two shots into the air, then ran to my car and came back home. I thought Marcia was in bed. But when, after a couple of hours, I went up, I found she wasn't there, that she had left that note. That's why I came to you. I wanted your help. That's the truth, so help me."

Mason said, "You wrote down the license number of that automobile. Later on you tried to cover it up by adding some words and some figures. Then you added the total—"

"Mr. Mason, I swear I did not."

"Who did then?"

"I don't know."

"Someone wrote down the license number of the car," Mason said, "4E4705, then tried to camouflage it by working in a number of other figures and writing at the top *These numbers called*—but a mistake was made in the addition. I . . . wait a minute . . ."

Mason stood motionless, his eyes level-lidded with concentration.

"Perhaps," Major Winnett suggested, "it was . . ."

Mason motioned him to silence, then, after a moment,

picked up the telephone, dialed the hotel where Drake had established an office, and when he had Drake on the line, said, "Hello, Paul. Perry talking. I think I've got it. There wasn't any mistake in the addition."

"I don't get it," Drake said. "The total should be 49″37818. Actually it's 49″37817."

"And that figure is right," Mason said. "The number we want is 4E4704."

"But the license number was 4E4705."

Mason said, "What happens when you have two cars? You are given license numbers in chronological order. Look up license number 4E4704. You can start your search in room six-thirteen there at the hotel. Make it snappy."

Mason slammed up the telephone receiver and nodded to Major Winnett. "We've got one more chance. It's slim. The next time you go to a lawyer, don't be so damn smart. Tell him the truth. Where's your mother's room?"

"In the other wing at the far end of the corridor."

"And the nurse's room?" Mason asked. "That must be a communicating room?"

"It is."

Mason said, "Let's go."

Helen Custer, answering their knock, seemed somewhat flustered. "Why, good evening. I, ah . . . is there something . . ."

Mason pushed his way into the room. Major Winnett hesitated a moment, then followed. Mason kicked the door shut.

"Police are on their way out here," Mason said to the nurse.

"The police? What for?"

"To arrest you."

"For what?"

Mason said, "That's up to you."

"What do you mean?"

Mason said, "Playing it one way, it's blackmail. Playing it the other way, it's being an accessory after the fact on a murder charge. You'd better take the rap for blackmail."

"I . . . I . . . why, *what* are you talking about?"

Mason said, "I've practiced law long enough to know that a man should never torture clues to make them point in the direction he thinks they should go. When that column of figures added up to 49E37817 and I thought it should have been 49E37818, I assumed a mistake had been made in the addition. It wasn't a mistake. You marked down the number *Cal* 4E4704. You wanted to preserve that number but you didn't want anyone to think that it had any significance, so you added the words at the top, *These numbers,* and then inserted *led* after the *Cal,* so that made it read, These numbers called. Then you added other numbers after that number and then totaled the sum. Now then, you probably have less than five minutes to tell us why you wrote down 4E4704."

She glanced from Mason to Major Winnett. There was dismay in her eyes. "What makes you think I—"

Mason took out his watch, said, "If the police get here first, you'll be an accessory after the fact. If you use your head, you *may* be able to get by with a rap for attempted blackmail."

"I . . . I . . . oh, Mr. Mason. I can't . . ."

Mason watched the hand ticking off the seconds.

"All right," she blurted. "It was yesterday morning. I was looking for Mrs. Victoria Winnett. I thought she was up in the observation tower. I went up there. She wasn't there. The binoculars were adjusted so they pointed down to that grove of trees. I just happened to look through them and saw the trailer. A light coupé was parked beside the big Buick that was attached to the trailer. A man and a woman were having a struggle of some sort. The man tried to strike her and the woman reached into her blouse. I saw the flash of a gun, then another flash. The man staggered back and the woman calmly closed the door of the trailer, got in her car and drove away.

"Through the binoculars I got a look at the number of her automobile. It was Cal 4E4704. I wrote it down on a piece of paper, intending to tell the police. Then . . . well, then I . . . thought . . . I . . . ."

"What did you do with the piece of paper?" Mason asked.

"After a moment I realized that perhaps I could . . . well, you know. So I changed the focus on the binoculars back to—"

"So what did you do?" Mason asked.

"I didn't want that number to seem too conspicuous. I had written Cal 4E4704, so I wrote down other things, just as you said."

"The first number you wrote on a single sheet of paper that was on the table and not on the pad. When you wrote the rest of it, you had placed the paper on the pad."

"I . . . I guess I did."

Mason pointed to the telephone. "Ring up police head-quarters," he said. "Tell them what you saw. Tell them that it's been bothering you, that you thought you should have re-ported it to the police, but that Mrs. Winnett is so opposed to any form of publicity that you didn't know just what to do; that tonight you asked Mrs. Winnett about it and she told you to telephone the police at once; that the reason you didn't do so before was because the trailer was gone when you looked again and you supposed that the man hadn't been hurt and had driven the trailer away."

"If I do that," she said, "then I . . . ."

"Then you stand about one chance in ten of beating the rap all around," Mason said grimly. "Don't do it, and you're stuck. What did you do—actually, I mean?"

"I looked up the license number. I found that the car was registered in the name of a Mrs. Harry Drummond. I located her, and while I wasn't crude or anything . . . I wanted to open up a beauty shop and . . . well, she agreed to finance me."

Once more Mason pointed to the telephone. "Get police headquarters. Come on, Major. Let's go."

Out in the corridor Major Winnett said, "But how about my wife, Mason? How about my wife? That's the thing that bothers me. That—"

"And it damned well should bother you," Mason said. "She must have seen you driving the trailer Wednesday night and followed you to the place where you parked it. She went in, found Drummond dead and thought you had been trying to avenge the family's good name. You can see now what happened. She gave Drummond money to get a divorce. He told her he'd secured one. She married again. Drummond made the mistake of also marrying again. When the blowoff came, his second wife threatened to prosecute him for bigamy unless he gave her money. The only way he had to get money was to put the heat on Marcia. She was too conscientious to ask you for money or to try to stick the insurance company for money, so she staged a fake burglary, cached her jewelry in the swallow's nest, then turned over the jewelry to him. When the second Mrs. Drummond came for her money, all her husband had to offer her was jewelry. She thought it was hot. That started a fight and she shot him. And probably shot him in self-defense at that."

"But how am I going to explain—about moving the body?" Major Winnett asked.

Mason looked at him pityingly. "You're not going to explain one damn thing," he said. "What do you think you have a lawyer for? Get in my car. Leave the nurse to put the police on a hot trail."

CHAPTER ELEVEN

IT WAS nearing midnight when Perry Mason and Paul Drake walked into metropolitan police headquarters with a description of Marcia Winnett and a series of photographs.

"Of course," Mason explained to Sergeant Dorset, "the major doesn't want any publicity. She had a spell of amnesia several years ago. He's afraid it *may* have returned."

Sergeant Dorset frowned down at a memo on his desk. "We've picked up a woman who answers that description—amnesia—a hospital telephoned in the report. How does it happen *you're* mixed in the case, Mason?"

"I handle the Winnetts' business."

"The deuce you do!"

"That's right."

Dorset regarded the memo on his desk. "The county teletype says a man named Drummond was murdered. Mrs. Winnett's nurse saw it all, phoned in a report. She had the license number of the murder car, Drummond's wife's."

"Indeed," Mason said, his voice showing courteous interest, but nothing else. "May we take a look at this amnesia case now? The major is very anxious."

"And," Dorset went on, "when the county officers picked up Drummond's wife, she swore that not only was the killing in self-defense, but that the nurse had been blackmailing her. The nurse called her a liar. Mrs. Drummond's confession puts her in a poor position to claim blackmail. I understand

the county is so pleased with having cracked the murder case
they're washing their hands of all the rest of it."

Mason glared at Sergeant Dorset. "Will you kindly tell me
what all this has to do with Major Winnett's wife?"

Dorset sighed. "I wish to hell I knew," he said, and then
added significantly, "but I'll bet a hundred to one we never
find out now."

Mason said, "Come down to earth. That murder case is
county. The sheriff's office wouldn't like a city dick sticking
his nose in."

Dorset nodded. "And by the same sign the way you've arranged it, the amnesia case is city and the county men won't
mess around with *that*."

He regarded the lawyer with a certain scowling respect.

Mason said very positively, "I don't see what the murder
has to do with all this if the sheriff's office has a solution and
a confession, but one thing I do know is that if you have
Major Winnett's wife here she's suffering from a nervous ail-
ment and if you make it worse with a lot of fool notions,
you'll wish you hadn't. Do I get her now, or do I get a *habeas
corpus?*"

"Hell, you get her now," Dorset said disgustedly. "I can't
help feeling that if I knew everything you'd been doing in
the last twelve hours I'd get a promotion, and if I try to find
out, I'll be back pounding pavements. Damn it!"

He picked up the telephone and said into the transmitter,
"Send that amnesia case number eighty-four on the night
bulletin up to my office."

The Candy Kid

LESTER LEITH, slender and debonair, gathered his lounging robe about him and sprawled at silken ease.

"Scuttle, the cigarettes."

His valet proffered the case of monogrammed cigarettes with a synthetic servility which ill became the massive hulk of the man.

"Yes, sir," he said.

"And the crime clippings. I think I'd like to read about crime."

The valet, who was in reality no valet at all, but a police spy employed to watch Leith and report his every move, let his thick lips twist into a grin.

"Yes, sir. I was going to speak to you about them. Your prediction has come true."

"My prediction, Scuttle?"

"Yes, sir. You remember Carter Mills, the gem expert?"

Lester Leith puckered his forehead.

"Mills . . . The name seems to be familiar, Scuttle. . . . Oh, yes, he was the one who was working on the ruby necklace for some rajah or other. He insisted on grabbing all the newspaper publicity he could get. I remember the headline: CARRIES A MILLION DOLLARS TO WORK."

The valet nodded. "Yes, sir. That's the one. You remember he had his photograph taken with a leather briefcase in his hand. The newspaper article mentioned that he carried a fortune in rare gems back and forth from his place of business to his house. He was making a design for the rubies, flanked with diamonds. It was to be something unique in the art of gem setting, sir, and—"

"Yes, yes, Scuttle. There's no need to go into it again, but you'll remember that I mentioned he was simply inviting danger."

"Yes, sir. You said that Mr. Mills didn't realize how businesslike the underworld had become. You mentioned that he would find himself robbed some day and that his client would find, to his grief, that it didn't pay to have a gem designer who carried a million dollars' worth of stones around in a briefcase."

Leith nodded. "I take it, Scuttle, that all this is merely a preface to telling me that Mr. Mills *was* robbed?"

"Yes, sir. Yesterday morning, sir. He went to work in a taxicab. He was carrying the briefcase stuffed with gems and sketches. When he opened his shop he found a man standing inside with a gun. The man ordered Mills to come in and lock the door, and Mills had to obey. The man took the briefcase and started to run for the back.

"But Mills hadn't been altogether foolish. He had installed a burglar alarm just inside the door, and he'd notified the occupants of adjoining buildings what it would mean when the burglar alarm sounded.

"He pressed the burglar alarm and then grabbed a shotgun which he kept behind the counter for just such an emergency. He fired, and he fired low. Some of the pellets hit the bandit's legs.

"The sound of the shots and the noise of the burglar alarm made a terrific commotion. You see, it was early in the morning. Mr. Mills makes a habit of being the first one to come to his shop every morning. I believe it was about ten minutes to eight, sir.

"But there were clerks in some of the adjoining stores, and there was a traffic officer on duty at the corner. Naturally, these men all got into action.

"By the time the bandit reached the alley there were two clerks waiting for him. He ran toward a car that was parked in the alley and started it. But the clerks shouted to the traffic officer and he sprinted for the mouth of the alley.

"The bandit saw him coming, jumped out of the car, still carrying the briefcase, and dashed into the rear door of a candy store."

Lester Leith held up his hand.

"Just a moment, Scuttle. You say he was wounded, this bandit?"

"Yes, sir."

"Bleeding, Scuttle?"

"Yes, sir."

"Clerks behind him raising an alarm?"

"Yes, sir, and Mr. Mills, with a shotgun, banging birdshot at him."

"Birdshot, Scuttle?"

"Yes, sir—a size they call Number Eight."

Lester Leith blew a meditative smoke ring at the raftered ceiling.

"Rather an unusual size of shot for a man to use in repelling a bandit, Scuttle!"

"Yes, sir, it is. But, as Mr. Mills explained to the police, one is less apt to miss with a charge of small shot. And he was most anxious, as he expressed it, to leave his marks on the bandit."

Lester Leith waved his hand in a careless gesture.

"Quite right, Scuttle. Number Eight shot will make a most

uniform pattern, and it's deadly if the range is short. What happened next?"

"Well, sir, the back door of the candy store was open, because the proprietor was moving out some boxes and refuse. But the store hadn't been opened for business, so the front door was locked.

"The proprietor of the candy store ran out and locked the back door. The bandit was trapped. It took a key to open the front door and the proprietor had taken that key with him when he ran out the back door.

"The police besieged the place with tear gas and machine guns. They killed the bandit, riddled him with bullets, sir."

Lester Leith nodded. "Recovered the gems and closed the case, I take it, Scuttle?"

"No, sir. That's the funny part of it. The bandit had fifteen or twenty minutes in the candy store, and he hid the stones so cleverly that the police haven't been able to find them. They recovered the briefcase, of course, and the penciled designs, and perhaps half a dozen loose stones. But there were literally dozens of the stones concealed so cleverly the police have been completely baffled.

"They identified the bandit. He was a man named Grigsby, known in the underworld as Griggy the Gat, and he had a long criminal record."

Lester Leith blew another smoke ring, extended the forefinger of his right hand, and traced the perimeter of the swirling smoke.

"I see, Scuttle. Then Griggy the Gat must have concealed the gems somewhere between Mills's shop and the candy store, or somewhere in the candy store, when he knew that capture was inevitable?"

"Yes, sir."

"And the police can't find them, you say, Scuttle?"

"No, sir. They've looked everywhere. They've searched

every inch of the candy store. They've even searched the car in which Griggy the Gat tried to make his escape from Mills's place. They simply can't find a single trace of the stones."

Lester Leith's eyes were bright now, and the valet watched him as a cat watches a mousehole.

"Scuttle, you interest me."

"Yes, sir."

"The candy shop was wholesale or retail, Scuttle?"

"Both, sir. It's a small factory too—in the rear, sir."

"And the rubies were worth a great deal of money, Scuttle?"

"Yes, sir. Of course, the newspaper account, valuing them at a million dollars, was exaggerated. But the rajah has offered a reward of twenty thousand dollars for their return."

Leith lapsed into thought once more. Finally he flipped the cigarette into the fireplace and chuckled.

"You've thought of something, sir?"

Lester Leith regarded the valet coldly.

"One always is thinking of something, Scuttle."

The valet's face turned brick-red.

"Yes, sir. I had thought perhaps you had worked out a solution, sir."

"Scuttle, are you crazy? How could I work out a solution of where the gems are?"

The valet shrugged. "You've done it before, sir."

"Done what before, Scuttle?"

"Solved intricate crime problems just from reading what the newspapers had to say about them."

Lester Leith laughed. "Tut, tut, Scuttle, you're getting as bad as Sergeant Ackley! Many times I've thought out *possible* solutions, but no more. True, Sergeant Ackley has a theory I must be guilty of something just because I take an interest in crime clippings. He keeps hounding me with his infernal activities, suspecting me of this, suspecting me of that. And he tortures the facts to make them fit his theories. Do you know, Scuttle, an impartial observer hearing Ackley's theories might come to the conclusion I was guilty of some crime or other."

Lester Leith watched his valet with narrowed eyes.

The valet, mindful of his duties as a valet, yet recollecting also that he was an undercover man for the police, and anxious to trap Lester Leith into some damaging admission, nodded sagely.

"Yes, sir. I've thought so myself at times."

"Thought what?"

"How convincing the sergeant's theories are, sir. You've got to admit that there's some mastermind who is doping out the solutions of baffling crimes in advance of the police. By the time the police solve the crime, this mastermind has scooped up the loot and gone. The police have only the empty satisfaction of solving the crime. They never recover the loot."

Lester Leith yawned prodigiously.

"And so Sergeant Ackley has convinced you that I'm that mastermind?"

The valet spoke cautiously, aware that he was treading on dangerous ground. "I didn't say so, sir. I merely mentioned that sometimes Sergeant Ackley's theories sound convincing."

Lester Leith lit another cigarette.

"Tut, tut, Scuttle. You should know better. If I were this mysterious criminal the sergeant talks so much about, it stands to reason I'd have been caught long ago. You must remember the sergeant has had shadows tail me everywhere I go. He's continually popped into the apartment with his wild accusations and submitted me to search. But he's never discovered a single shred of evidence. Surely he'd have had some proof by this time if he were at all correct."

The valet shrugged again. "Perhaps, sir."

"Perhaps, Scuttle! You don't sound at all convinced by my line of reasoning."

"Well, sir, you must remember that it's the most difficult sort of a crime to prove—the robbing of robbers. Naturally, the one who is robbed doesn't dare to complain, since to do so would brand *him* as a criminal."

"Pshaw, Scuttle. Your reasoning is getting to be like that of the police. Besides, I think the sergeant is making a mistake."

"How so, sir?"

"In concentrating so much on the hijacker that he lets the real criminals slip away. After all, this mysterious mastermind of the sergeant's, no matter who he may be, is a public benefactor."

"A benefactor, sir?"

"Certainly, Scuttle. If we concede the man exists outside the imagination of Sergeant Ackley, we must admit that he makes it his business to detect crimes in time to strip the criminal of his ill-gotten gains. That's all society would do with the criminal if Sergeant Ackley apprehended him. The court would confiscate his loot, perhaps imprison him, but too often some slick lawyer would get him off."

"Perhaps, sir."

"No doubt about it, Scuttle!"

"No, sir, perhaps not. But you must admit that you have a mysterious trust fund which keeps growing, sir. True, that trust fund is administered for needy widows and orphans, but I understand the fund has grown so large that you have to employ a clerical staff to handle its disbursements."

Lester Leith's eye glittered.

"Indeed, Scuttle. And where did you get such detailed information about my private affairs?"

"Sergeant Ackley," blurted the valet. "He insisted on stopping me on the street and telling me his suspicions. He thinks you are just the type of man who would enjoy doping out crime solutions, levying tribute from the criminal, and then turning the money into a trust fund for the unfortunate."

Lester Leith began to laugh. "The dear sergeant! The overzealous, stupid, blundering incompetent! But we have digressed. We were talking about Mills, Griggy the Gat, and a million dollars' worth of rare gems. Do you know, Scuttle, the crime *does* interest me. How thoroughly have the police searched?"

"I understand, from the newspapers and from gossip, that they searched every nook and cranny. They probed between walls. They poked under showcases, they looked in sugar bins, they poured out barrels of syrup. They took the upholstering of the bandit's automobile to pieces."

"Did they look in the candy, Scuttle?"

"Where?"

"In the candy."

"Why—er—that is, I don't know what you mean, sir. How could one look inside of candy and how could a man hide gems in candy?"

"There were chocolate creams in this candy factory, Scuttle?"

"Yes, sir."

"It would be readily possible for a man to melt off the chocolate coating and thrust in one or two gems."

"But the candy would show it had been tampered with, sir."

"Not if it was redipped. By the way, Scuttle, go to this candy place and see if you can buy some of the chocolate creams that were on the upper floor of the establishment when the fighting was going on. I should like to examine them."

"Yes, sir. How many, sir?"

"Oh, quite a good supply. Say around fifty dollars' worth. And find out if there was any dipping chocolate that was warm while the bandit was cornered in the place.

"You see, Scuttle, the problem fascinates me. There are so many places in a candy store or factory where gems might be hidden. The proprietor may get his chocolate shipped to him in large thick bars. What would prevent a criminal from melting a hole in a bar of chocolate, dropping in some stones, and then sealing up the chocolate with a little dipping chocolate?

"Of course, Scuttle, I'm only interested in a theoretical solution, you understand. I don't want actually to recover the gems. I only want to see if they *could* have been hidden that way.

"Now, Scuttle, I don't want any trouble about this. Telephone Sergeant Ackley and ask him if there is any possible objection to my buying candy from the store in which the bandit was killed."

The valet's mouth sagged. "Now, sir?"

"Oh, no great hurry, Scuttle. You might even drop by and ask the sergeant for his opinion. See if you can get him to scribble a note stating there's no objection on the part of the police department to my purchasing candy.

"Better run along and buy the chocolates, Scuttle—and also get me an electric soldering iron. Oh, yes, Scuttle, and you'd better get some of those hard, red cinnamon drops too."

The valet-spy oozed his huge bulk from the room, clapped a hat on his head, and opened the outer door.

"Right away, sir. I shall carry out your orders to the letter, sir."

Sergeant Arthur Ackley scraped a spadelike thumbnail over the coarse stubble along the angle of his jaw. Across the table sat Edward H. Beaver, undercover man assigned to Lester Leith. The undercover man had just finished his report and Sergeant Ackley was considering it, his crafty eyes filmed with thought.

"Beaver," he said at length, "I'm going to let you in on something. We've recovered four of the rubies."

"Found them?" asked the undercover man.

Sergeant Ackley shook his head. He took a box of perfectos from the drawer of his desk and selected one, without offering the box to the man opposite.

"No, we didn't find them. We recovered them. Two were given to a girl and pawned. One was handed to a man who was mooching, and the other was dropped in the cup of a blind beggar."

Beaver's lips parted in astonishment.

"Fact. Girl named Molly Manser was standing looking at a window. She says a heavyset man with a hat pulled low over his forehead and a patch over his left eye sidled up to her and asked her if she'd like some of the clothes on display in the window.

"She says she tried to walk away, but he grabbed her arm and pushed a couple of the rubies into her hand. She claims she broke away and ran, but the man didn't try to follow her."

Beaver twisted his lips. "Boloney," he said. "What did she do with 'em?"

"Took 'em to Gildersmith to hock."

"He knew they were hot?"

"Sure. He spotted 'em and held her until one of our men got there. Mills identified 'em instantly; says he can't be fooled on those rubies."

Beaver sighed. "Then she was one of the gang and they've managed to find out where the gems were and take 'em."

"Wait a minute," said Sergeant Ackley. "You're behind the times. We figured that, of course, and put the girl in the cooler. Half an hour later another pawnbroker telephoned in he had a ruby he wanted us to look at. We went out on the run. It was the same size, same color, same kind of cutting.

"This time a down-and-outer had brought it in. He was a panhandler, mooching the price of a drink. He picked on a heavyset guy with a hat pulled well down and a patch over the right eye. The guy told him to take the stone, hock it, and keep whatever he got out of it.

"Then, while we were questioning this guy, the telephone gave us another lead—a blind beggar who had one of the stones dropped into his cup. Naturally, he couldn't see who did it, but he heard the sound of the man's steps on the sidewalk. He said it was a heavyset man.

"Now that sort of puts a different slant on this candy idea, eh?"

The undercover man nodded slowly. "Maybe I'd better switch him to some other crime."

Sergeant Ackley shook his head emphatically.

"Somehow or other, those four rubies slipped through. We want to find out where and when. This guy, Leith, never has missed a bet yet. If we can use him as a hound to smell out the trail we can kill two birds with one stone.

"Besides, Mills is raising hell. He's related to one of the political big shots, and he's riding us up one side and down the other. That's just like his type. They smear publicity all over the papers that they're carrying a million dollars around with them and then squawk when they get rolled."

Beaver teetered back and forth in the scarred chair. His brow was corrugated in thought.

"Sergeant," he suddenly whispered.

Sergeant Ackley scowled at him. "Well?"

"Sergeant," said Beaver, "I have it. I tell you I *have* it—a scheme to frame Lester Leith! We'll get the candy, just like he said. You've got four of the rubies that were stolen. Those rubies can't be told from any of the other stolen rubies. We'll plant those rubies in the candy and hand 'em to Leith.

"After a while Leith will find those rubies. He'll salt 'em. We'll be watching him all the time and we'll nab him for possession of stolen property, for being an accessory after the fact, and"—Beaver clenched and unclenched the hamlike fist of his right hand—"for resisting an officer!"

Sergeant Ackley grinned. "Make it for resisting two officers, Beaver," and he doubled up his own right fist.

"It'll be a cinch," said Beaver. "He's got off wrong on this case and thinks the rubies are hidden in the candy. But we don't care how right or how wrong he is, just so we can get him with stolen property."

Sergeant Ackley shot his open hand across the table.

"Shake, Beaver! By George, I'll see that you get a promotion for this! It's an idea that'll stick Mr. Lester Leith inside, lookin' out."

Beaver shook hands.

"Of course, it'll be framing him," he said.

Sergeant Ackley snorted. "Who cares, just so we get him!"

Beaver nodded solemnly.

"All right. I'll get the candy and come back here. We'll plant the rubies. You'd better write me a note I can take to him so he'll feel I've got results. Say in the note he can buy anything he pleases so far as the department is concerned."

Sergeant Ackley squinted one eye. "It's sort of a fool letter to write."

"I know, but it will make Leith think I'm on the level with him."

Ackley nodded. "Go on out and pick up the candy. Bring it back here and we'll stick in the rubies."

It took Beaver an hour to get the candy and the soldering iron and return to headquarters. Sergeant Ackley was pacing the floor in the manner of a caged lion.

"Took you long enough, Beaver," he grunted. "Let's get busy."

"The candy in the boxes?" asked Beaver.

"Yeah. Put the rubies in the top row, one in each of four boxes. Mark the boxes and mark the candies that have the rubies in 'em. I've thought of a slick way of getting the rubies into the candy. We simply heat the rubies in a pan. Then, when they're warm, press 'em against the bottoms of the chocolates and let 'em melt in."

Beaver nodded appreciatively.

"Beats Leith's idea of the soldering iron," he agreed.

Sergeant Ackley sneered. "Leith ain't so brainy. He's just had the breaks, that's all. This idea of mine is going to put him where he belongs."

"My idea," corrected Beaver.

Sergeant Ackley scowled. "I'll let you have some of the credit, Beaver, but don't try to hog things. I thought of the idea. That is, I outlined the whole thing and was just pointing out to you how to handle it when you interrupted and took the words out of my mouth."

Beaver's jaw dropped.

They found an alcohol stove and a pan. They heated the rubies and picked up a chocolate. One of the hot rubies was pushed through the bottom of the chocolate.

Sergeant Ackley surveyed the result.

"Not so good. Looks kinda messy," he said.

"We can take this electric soldering iron and sort of smooth it over," said Beaver.

Ackley nodded. "Watch out. Your fingers are melting the

chocolate, leaving fingerprints on it. We don't want that. Better wear gloves. That's the way they do it in the candy factories."

They heated the iron and held it against the chocolate. When they had finished, the result was hardly artistic.

"Well," said Sergeant Ackley, "I guess it'll get by. But we won't need to mark the chocolates that have the gems in them."

"No," agreed the undercover man.

Beaver picked up the carton containing the boxes of chocolates. The last word he heard as he sidled out of Ackley's private office was a petulant comment from the sergeant.

"I'm not so sure, Beaver, that idea of yours is any good."

Lester Leith beamed on the undercover man.

"Well, well, Scuttle, you have had a busy afternoon, haven't you? And you've done nobly—the candy, the soldering iron, even a letter from Sergeant Ackley written on police stationery, stating that I can buy anything I want. That's fine!

"Now let's see if I can melt one of the candies and insert one of the red cinnamon drops. We'll pretend that the cinnamon drop represents a ruby."

Leith connected the electric soldering iron and set to work. When he was finished, there was chocolate smeared over his fingers, his face was flushed, and three chocolate creams were now sloppy and formless.

"How long did this Griggy the Gat have in the candy shop, Scuttle?"

"Not more than fifteen or twenty minutes, sir."

"Then he couldn't have done it, Scuttle."

"Couldn't have done what, sir?"

"Hid the gems in the candy."

"Begging your pardon, sir. Couldn't he have done a better job if he'd heated the stones and pressed them into the chocolate, and then finished the job with the hot iron?"

Lester Leith stared at his man with narrowed eyes. "Scuttle, have you been experimenting?"

"Not exactly, sir. That is to say, no, sir. And by the way, sir, while I think of it, I picked up a bit of gossip at headquarters. It seems four of the stones have been found by the police."

The valet told Leith how the four stones were recovered.

When he had finished, Lester Leith was chuckling. "Scuttle, that's all the information I needed to give me a perfect solution to the crime."

"Yes, sir?"

"Yes, Scuttle. But of course, you understand it's only a theoretical solution, and I do not intend to put it to any practical use."

"Of course, sir."

"And now I have some errands for you before the stores close. I want you to get me four genuine pearls of the finest luster. I want a package of cornstarch. I want some quick-drying cement and some powdered alum."

The valet was rubbing his jaw.

"And, Scuttle," said Lester Leith, beaming, "you've heard of daylight saving, of course. What do you think of it?"

"It's inconvenient in the mornings, sir, but convenient in the evening."

"Yes, indeed, Scuttle. Yet a moment's thought will convince you that it hasn't saved any daylight. It's merely kidded man into believing that there is more daylight. The days aren't any longer. Man simply gets up earlier."

"Yes, sir. I guess so, sir."

"Yes, indeed, Scuttle. But it's a great plan. However, we

shouldn't limit it to clock juggling. Why not carry it to its
logical conclusion and have a heat-saving plan? Why not
have perpetual summer?"

The valet was interested, but dazed.

"How could you do that, sir?"

"I'll show you. It's now the second of November."

"Yes, sir."

"Very well, Scuttle. You see that calendar hanging against
the wall?"

"Yes, sir."

"Watch it."

And Lester Leith, stepping to the calendar, tore off the
month of November. He did the same for December. Next
year's calendar was underneath, and from this he removed
January, February, March, April, May, and June. The
month that remained on top was July.

"There we are, Scuttle. We simply set the calendar ahead
eight months. We now have summer with us. See, according
to the calendar it's July second. Think of what that means to
suffering humanity. Summer is here, and we haven't had a
single cold spell. Winter is over! Rejoice, Scuttle!"

The valet-spy sank into a chair.

"Have you gone stark raving mad?" he demanded.

"No," said Lester Leith, pursing his lips judiciously, "I
think not, Scuttle. Why do you suggest it?"

"But, good Lord, sir, simply tearing off the calendar won't
make summer come any quicker."

"Why, you surprise me, Scuttle. You admit daylight saving
gives us an hour more of daylight."

"Well, that's different. You said yourself it was merely a
scheme by which men kid themselves."

"Certainly, Scuttle. And that's all tearing off the leaves of
the calendar does. Come, come, Scuttle, enter into the spirit
of the thing. It's the second of July, and you've got the heat

on. Shut the heat off, and then start out and get me the pearls and the cornstarch and the alum, and quick-drying cement. And you had better get a small crucible and a blowtorch too.

"Some of the things you'll have to pay cash for, Scuttle. The pearls you can charge. Get them at Hendricksen's, and he can telephone me for an okay on the order if he wishes. But get started, Scuttle. Even in these long summer days the stores close promptly at five o'clock."

"It isn't summer, sir, it's the second day of November."

"Tut, tut, Scuttle, don't be such an old fossil! Adapt yourself to the times!"

The valet, shaking his head, shut off the steam heat and slipped from the apartment. Lester Leith opened the windows, and the cold of the late November afternoon crept into the room.

From a public telephone booth Scuttle reported to Sergeant Ackley and his report sounded strangely garbled.

Sergeant Ackley muttered a curse over the wire. "Beaver, you've been drinking."

"No, sir, I haven't. I swear I haven't had a drop. Go on out there and see for yourself, if you don't believe me. I tell you he's gone crazy. He had me shutting off the heat just before I left. And he insists that it's July according to this crazy calendar saving time of his. Go there, if you don't believe it."

"By George, I *will* go out there!" yelled Sergeant Ackley.

Which was why, as Lester Leith sat bundled to the ears in a fur coat, there was an imperative rap on the door. He arose and opened it.

Sergeant Ackley glared at him. "H'lo, Leith. Happened to be in the neighborhood and dropped in to see you."

Lester Leith gathered the fur coat about him.

"Is this an official visit, Sergeant?"

"Well, not exactly."

"You haven't a warrant either for search or arrest?"

"Good Lord, no! I tell you I just dropped in."

"Very well, then, it's a social visit. Do come in, Sergeant, and sit down. It's a little chilly for July. In fact, I don't re-member when there's been a cooler summer."

The sergeant stared at Lester Leith. "A cooler summer! Dammit, man, it's winter."

Lester Leith positively beamed. "By George, that's so. I forgot to tell you of my new heat-saving scheme. It's the same as daylight saving. That is, it depends on the same psycholog-ical factors, and it's equally logical.

"You see, like every great idea, it's simple. We achieve day-light saving simply by setting our clocks ahead. Well, I've achieved heat saving by the same method. I've set the calendar ahead. I tear off eight months and make it July. It's marvelously simple!"

Sergeant Ackley peered intently at Lester Leith.

"You're cuckoo," he said. "It's freezing in here. You'll catch your death of cold. Good Lord, sitting in a room with the windows all up and the thermometer down to freezing!"

Sergeant Ackley sat on the edge of a chair and shivered.

"Hello, what's the idea of all the candy?" he asked.

"Just a whim, Sergeant. I was thinking about that unfortu-nate robbery of Mr. Mills, and I wondered if it was possible that the criminal had concealed the rubies in some of the candy."

"So you sent out and bought this candy. Did it ever occur to you that you'd have been in rather a bad position if the candy *had* contained the gems?"

Lester Leith smiled frankly.

"Of course, Sergeant. That's why I had my man call on you and get permission in writing to purchase anything he wanted."

Sergeant Ackley's brows knitted.

"But it was all a mistake. The hiding couldn't have been worked that way. Have a piece of candy, Sergeant."

Lester Leith extended a box and the sergeant took a chocolate, taking care to inspect the bottom before he sank his teeth into it.

For several seconds he toyed with the candy, going through the motions of eating it, yet making little headway. All of a sudden he stiffened and looked at the candy between his forefinger and thumb. Then he looked at the insides of the thumb and forefinger and sat upright in his chair.

"Something?" asked Lester Leith politely.

But Sergeant Ackley was halfway to the door.

"You devil!" he exclaimed. "You clever devil!"

And the door banged behind him.

Lester Leith gazed at the door with a puzzled frown.

Sergeant Ackley sprinted for the elevator and literally ran into Beaver at the sidewalk. He shot out a huge hand and scooped Beaver into an alcove.

"He ain't crazy," said Sergeant Ackley. "I don't know what his game is, but it's the cleverest scheme ever pulled in a criminal case."

Beaver, his arms filled with packages, surveyed his superior with blinking eyes.

"Have *you* gone daffy, too?"

Sergeant Ackley shook his head.

"Look here," he said, "when we heated the gems and tried to put them in the chocolate creams, what happened?"

"Why, we messed the job up," admitted Beaver.

"Right," said Sergeant Ackley. "Chocolate melts at about the heat of the human blood, see? Well, if you hadn't been such a damned fool you'd have remembered the room was steam-heated. That's what made the chocolates messy! Now Lester Leith is sitting up there with the heat off and the windows open. The room is freezing. But look what it did to the chocolates! You can hold one of them in your fingers for minutes and it won't get sloppy. You could slip a hot stone into those chocolates and cover up the place by holding a hot iron near the chocolate, and make a perfect job of it. And you could do it quick!"

The valet-spy's jaw sagged.

"Of course! And the loft of the candy store was cold when Griggy the Gat was in there!"

Sergeant Ackley nodded. "I'm glad to see that you're not entirely hopeless, Beaver. Now you get up to that apartment and humor Lester Leith in this heat-saving idea of his. Give him all the rope he wants. Put on an overcoat and let the room get just as cold as he wants it. And be sure to keep your eye on that candy!"

"How about the candy that's still out at the candy factory?"

Sergeant Ackley chuckled. "That's where I'm going right now. I'm going to have the police buy up every ounce of that candy, all the chocolate and all the mixing cream, and I'm going to put them all in one great big pot and melt them down. Then I'm going to pour off the syrup and see what's left. I have an idea we'll have the rest of those gems!"

"Meaning," asked Beaver, "that there are stones in the candy upstairs?"

Sergeant Ackley nodded.

"And we spent the afternoon putting more stones in it!"

"That," snapped Sergeant Ackley, "was *your* idea, Beaver. Now go up there and watch him like a hawk. When we get ready to spring the trap we'll spring it right."

When Beaver entered the apartment, Lester Leith was wrapped in a fur overcoat, his ankles covered with a wool blanket.

"Ah, good evening, Scuttle. Back already. Do you know,

Scuttle, I can't remember ever having seen a colder summer!"

The valet peered at the calendar.

"Here it is July already, and cold. Sometimes June is rather cool, but it's unusual July weather, sir."

Lester Leith smiled and nodded. "Very well spoken. You got the things for me?"

The valet nodded.

Lester Leith idly reached for a chocolate cream. The valet watched him intently.

Lester Leith's hand went to his mouth. He pushed some red object into the palm of his hand with his tongue, and his face lit with a smile of satisfaction.

The valet knew it was not one of the pieces he and Sergeant Ackley had loaded with the four rubies, so he leaned forward eagerly.

"Something, sir?" he asked, his voice trembling.

Lester Leith dropped the red object into his pocket.

"Yes, Scuttle, one of the red cinnamon drops. I forgot that I had put them in the chocolates, and cinnamon drops don't mix very well with cream."

There was a knock on the door. The valet eased his bulk toward the door and opened it. A dark-haired young woman with a very red mouth stood on the threshold. Her eyes were sparkling from the crisp air of the winter night.

"Which one of you is Lester Leith?" she asked.

Leith got to his feet as the girl walked into the cold room and the valet closed the door.

"Heat off?" asked the girl.

Lester Leith held a chair for her.

"Yes," he said. "I am trying an experiment in heat saving."

"Well, you're saving it all right. . . . All right, what are you giving away?"

Leith explained to his valet. "I telephoned a friend of

mine and told him I had a gift for a deserving young lady."
Then turning to their visitor, he said, "I want to give you
some candy. I made a rather large candy purchase on a specu-
lation which didn't turn out, and I'm left with the candy on
my hands."

The valet-spy said, "You wouldn't give it away, sir—"

Lester Leith said coldly, "That will do, Scuttle." He
turned again to the girl. "If you think your—er—boyfriend
would misinterpret the spirit which prompts this gift, I
should be glad to deliver it to you in his presence."

The girl's eyes narrowed.

Leith continued, "I'll carry the candy down to a cab."

She was sizing him up with eyes accustomed to make fast
and accurate appraisals. In the end she reached the verdict
which most women reached with Lester Leith.

"Okay," she said.

Leith loaded his arms with candy boxes and escorted the
woman to the door.

"I'll help you carry some of the boxes down, sir," said Scuttle.

Lester Leith shook his head. "You stay right here, Scuttle."

And he led the way to the elevator, made two more trips
back for candy, and then wished the police spy a good night.

"You'll be back soon, sir?" asked the valet, noticing that
Lester Leith had evening clothes under his overcoat.

Lester Leith smiled. "Scuttle," he said, "I am an opportunist."

And the outer door clicked as the springlock shot into
place.

The spy made a lunge for the telephone, where he called
Sergeant Ackley and poured out a report which made the
sergeant mutter exclamations of anger.

"Dammit, Beaver, he couldn't have given away *all* the
candy!"

"But he did."

"And he went with her?"

"Yes."

"Well, I've got shadows on the job. They'll tail him."

"Yes, Sergeant, I know, but how about the candy? The shadows will tail Leith, but they won't tail the girl after Leith leaves her. She'll have the candy, and the candy's got a bunch of rubies and diamonds in it—"

"Damn that fool idea of *yours*, Beaver. Get down and tell those shadows to forget Leith and tail the candy. Get me, tail that *candy*."

But by the time Beaver reached the sidewalk there was no trace of Leith, the girl, or the candy. Nor, of course, of the shadows. Following instructions, they had tailed Lester Leith.

It was well past midnight when Lester Leith returned. He scowled at his valet.

"Tut, tut, Scuttle, you have turned the heat on! Here I work out a new calendar arrangement that's to be a boon to mankind, and you spoil it all. It's July, Scuttle! One doesn't have steam heat on in July!"

The valet could only raise his tired eyes.

Leith softened. "Scuttle, I'll have some errands for you to do in the morning."

"Yes, sir."

"Ring up Sergeant Ackley and tell him I have a valuable clue on the Mills robbery. Then I want you to remember our patriotic obligations."

"Patriotic obligations, sir?"

"Quite right, Scuttle. Notice the date."

"It's the second—no, it's the third of November."

"No, no, it's the third of July! And on the fourth we celebrate the anniversary of the independence of our country. I shall want some firecrackers, Scuttle, and some slow-match—

'punk,' I think it's called. You can get them all at one of the Chinese stores. They keep firecrackers, not as seasonal merchandise, but as a staple."

"Lord, sir, are you really going to celebrate the fourth of July on the fourth of November?"

"Certainly, Scuttle. I presume you are not attempting to criticize me?"

"No, sir. I shall attend to the matter in the morning, sir."

"That's fine, Scuttle, and I wish you'd get me a siren."

"A what?"

"One of the electric sirens such as are used on police cars, Scuttle."

"But it's against the law to have one on your car unless you're an officer, sir."

"I didn't say anything about putting it on my car. I merely said I wanted one."

The valet nodded, then left, his expression more puzzled than ever.

For more than an hour Leith sat and smoked. From time to time he nodded his head as if he were checking the moves in a complicated game.

At the end of an hour he chuckled.

The morning was still young when Lester Leith was aroused by his valet.

"I'm sorry, sir, but it's Sergeant Ackley. You remember you told me to tell him you had a clue on the Mills robbery? Well, sir, Sergeant Ackley wouldn't wait. He's in the apartment now."

Leith stretched and yawned.

"Quite right, Scuttle. The sergeant is only doing his duty. Show him in."

The valet opened the door and Sergeant Ackley strode into the room.

"Well," said the sergeant. "What's the dope on Mills?"

Leith sat up. "You doubtless know, Sergeant, that I sent my valet for some candy to the same firm where Griggy the Gat was killed after the robbery. I had a theory that the thief might have put some of the stones in the candy, and—"

Sergeant Ackley rubbed his tired, red-rimmed eyes.

"Well, you can forget that! Thanks to that idea of yours, I had my men put in most of the night melting down every bit of candy and chocolate in the place. And we got nothing— absolutely nothing!"

"Did you now?" said Lester Leith. "That's strange, because I gave away my candy last night to a very beautiful young lady. When I left her she insisted that I eat some candy, and would you believe it, Sergeant, when I bit into that piece of candy there were three foreign substances in the filling!"

Sergeant Ackley's cigar drooped.

"Three!" he yelled.

"Yes, Sergeant, three. One of them was a cinnamon drop I'd put in myself earlier in the evening when I was experimenting, and the other two were red stones. I feel quite certain they are rubies. And I'm wondering, Sergeant, if perhaps they aren't some of the stolen loot."

Lester Leith reached in the pocket of his pajamas and took out a handkerchief. In this handkerchief was a knot which, on being loosened, revealed two large rubies of such deep fire and so perfectly matched that they looked like two drops of jeweled pigeon blood.

"Both in the *same* piece of candy?" asked Sergeant Ackley.

"Both in the same piece, Sergeant."

Sergeant Ackley framed his next question with a carelessness that was far too elaborate.

"Don't know where the girl is? The one that you gave the candy to?"

Lester Leith shook his head.

The sergeant turned to the door. "Going to see her again?"

Lester Leith shrugged. Then he said brightly, "You want to help me celebrate the fourth, Sergeant?"

"The fourth?"

"Of July, you know."

"Why, dammit, this is November."

"Oh, no, Sergeant, this is July. My new calendar calls—"

"Oh, hell!" stormed the sergeant, and slammed the door behind him.

Outdoors, he called the police shadows and gave them instructions.

"Tail Leith until he brings you to the candy or to the girl that's got the candy. After that, drop Leith and tail the candy. Get me? I want that candy!"

The police shadows saluted and returned to their stations. They waited for more than an hour before Lester Leith emerged.

Nor was it any secret to Lester Leith that the police shadows were waiting for him. He walked up to them.

"Gentlemen, good morning. So you won't have any trouble following me, I am going to get a taxicab. I will go directly to the Mills shop, where I will talk with Mr. Mills, the gentleman who was robbed. If you should lose me at any stage of the journey you can go directly there."

In the Mills shop Lester Leith became all business.

"Mr. Mills, what would you say to a process which produced wonderful pearls at a small cost? The best experts would swear they were genuine."

Mr. Carter Mills was a heavyset man with an undershot jaw and a leering eye.

"Nonsense," he said. "You're just another fool with another synthetic pearl scheme. Get out!"

Lester Leith took a pearl from his pocket and rolled it across the desk.

"Keep that as a souvenir of my visit," he said.

The jeweler picked up the pearl between his thumb and forefinger and was about to throw it away when he caught sight of the smooth sheen. He opened a drawer, took out a magnifying glass, and focused it on the pearl. Then he pressed a button on the side of his desk.

Lester Leith lit a cigarette.

The door of the private office opened and a man entered.

"Markle," snapped Mills, "take a look at this and tell me what it is."

The man nodded to Lester Leith, took a glass from his pocket, accepted the pearl from Mills, and studied it attentively. After nearly a minute Markle pronounced his verdict.

"It's a genuine pearl. Luster is good and it has a good shape."

Mills took the pearl from the man's cupped hand and jerked an authoritative thumb toward the door. Markle nodded once more to Leith and glided through the door.

Mills's eyes turned to Leith.

"You try to run a bunco on me and I'll have you jugged!"

Lester Leith took from his pocket a little globule of dead-looking white substance. It was, in fact, a combination of cornstarch and alum, dissolved in quick-drying waterproof cement.

"What's that?" asked the jeweler.

"Another pearl—or it will be when I've subjected it to my special process."

Mills examined it under the magnifying glass.

"Huh," he said. "There isn't any money in selling synthetic pearls."

"What's more, I haven't any money to put into equipment," said Leith.

The jeweler grinned. "All right. Let's have it."

"You will announce," said Lester Leith, "that you have found a wonderful pearl deposit off the Mexican coast. That deposit will be there, and your divers will actually bring up the pearls. But I will have first planted those pearls where the divers will find them. We will market the pearls at ridiculously low prices, and then, at the proper moment, sell the pearl bed."

Mills blinked his eyes. "You mean to salt a pearl mine?"

"And rake in a few million profit from doing it."

Mills looked shrewdly at Leith.

"It's illegal," he said. "If we were caught we would be jailed for fraud."

"If we were caught," admitted Leith.

The jeweler clasped his hands across his stomach. "How would you keep from getting caught?"

"I," said Lester Leith, "would keep you completely in the background. You would simply give me sufficient money to salt the field. I would plant pearls in the oysters. Then I would communicate with you and you would discover the field. You would be perfectly safe."

"What made you come to me?"

"I read of your loss of the rajah's gems in the paper. I knew the publicity would result unfavorably for you and that your legitimate business would suffer for a while. It occurred to me you might be interested."

Mills squinted his eyes. "Yet, after what you've told me, you don't dare to go to anyone else."

"Why?"

"I'd know too much. I could expose the deal."

Lester Leith smiled. "That's supposing you turn it down. You're not such a fool as to pass up millions of dollars in order to keep me from putting across a deal with someone else."

Mills sighed. "I'll look into the process and see how it works."

Lester Leith nodded. "I'll meet you anywhere you want tomorrow morning and give you a complete demonstration."

Mills got to his feet. "Tomorrow morning at nine o'clock at my house. I don't do important business here. There are too many eyes and ears. My house is my castle. Here's the address."

Lester Leith took the card.

"Tomorrow at nine."

Lester Leith loaded his car with a miscellaneous assortment of things which seemed to have no connection with each other. There was a suitcase containing the blowtorch and the crucible. There was a package of cornstarch, one of powdered alum, and one of waterproof, quick-drying cement. There was another suitcase containing firecrackers.

There was a siren, a battery, and an electrical connection. There were pliers and wires. There was, in fact, such a weird assortment as to make it seem that Lester Leith was going in the junk business.

But the police knew the unusual methods by which Lester Leith had managed in the past to solve crimes and hijack the criminals, and they watched Leith with cautious eyes.

And always the shadows were mindful of their instructions —whenever Leith should meet the girl, the shadows were to drop Leith and tail the candy.

If Leith knew of their instructions, he gave no sign. He drove the car down the boulevard, trailed by a police car.

The shadows were the best in the business. Yet the sedan which slipped between them and Lester Leith had been there for several blocks before the police realized that the two people in the sedan were also tailing Lester Leith.

The police dropped back.

The three cars threaded their way through the crowded

streets and came at length to a more open stretch of the coun-
tryside. Leith's car gathered speed. The sedan rushed close
behind it, and the police were forced to push the needle high
up on their speedometer to keep their quarry in sight.

Lester Leith slowed his car at a place where there was a vacant stretch of field, a bordering strip of woods, and a stone
wall.

The sedan also slid to a stop.

The roadside was deserted. For the police to have stopped
in that particular place would have meant they must disclose
their identity, so they slipped past the parked cars. But they
slowed their speed enough so that they could see just who it
was Leith was talking with.

And what they saw brought smiles to their faces. For Lester Leith was talking with the girl who had called at his
apartment, and the man with her was undoubtedly her boyfriend. But, what was more to the point, the two men in the
police car glimpsed boxes of candy in the rear of the sedan.

The detectives piloted their car around a curve in the
road, then slipped into the shelter of a stone wall. A pair of
powerful binoculars gave them a good view of what was taking place.

Lester Leith seemed very well acquainted. The man was
not quite as smiling as the girl, but the girl was effusively
cordial. After an interval of conversation a flask was
produced, also a picnic lunch. The trio ate lunch while the
detectives made notes of exactly what was happening.

Following lunch, the detectives received a surprise. Their
instructions had been to shadow Leith to the candy, and
after that to follow the candy until it was possible to communicate with Sergeant Ackley. But Ackley had advised them
that it was a million-to-one shot that Leith would never separate himself from that candy.

Yet Leith climbed into his car and drove down the road,

directly toward the detectives. The girl and her escort got into their sedan and drove back toward town.

There was no doubt as to the detectives' instructions. They took after the sedan.

The sedan hit the through boulevard some ten miles from town and started along it, traveling at a steady rate of speed.

"Looks like they're going right in, Louie," said the officer at the wheel. "I better drop you at the corner. Telephone headquarters, then stop a car and catch up with me."

The police car came to a stop before a drugstore, the shadow jumped to the ground, and was gone.

He notified Sergeant Ackley of the separation of Leith and the candy.

The sergeant got the location of the cars and their probable course, and ordered the shadow to get back to his companion as quickly as possible.

Within six miles, after commandeering a passing car, the detective rejoined his partner.

The cars continued their journey. The first important cross street brought them to a stop. Another police car slipped from the curb and the two shadows identified the sedan ahead by making signs.

What followed was short and snappy. The second police car forged ahead and abreast of the sedan. There was the sound of a siren, the motioning of uniformed arms, and the sedan slid to the curb. The driver leaned out to shout comments.

"Can't help it," said the officer in charge. "You folks have been driving recklessly. You'll have to come to headquarters and explain it to the sergeant. Bill, get over there in the sedan and see that they follow."

One of the officers pushed the candy boxes to one side and sat down on the rear seat.

At headquarters in the private office of Sergeant Ackley,

the sergeant gazed shrewdly at the captives before turning his eyes to the candy.

"Come through and come clean," he said.

"What," asked the man, "is the real charge?"

"Robbery."

"*What?*"

"You've got close to a million dollars' worth of stolen gems concealed in that candy."

There could be no mistaking their genuine astonishment.

"You got those boxes from a chap named Leith," said Ackley, "and the candy in them is loaded with the rubies and diamonds stolen from Mills."

The sergeant opened a box, bit into a piece of chocolate, chewed it up, and muttered his surprise as he found nothing except chocolate and cream filling. He bit into another, and the frown left his face. He twisted his tongue around, held his cupped hand before his mouth, and pushed a red object into the palm.

"Here's one of 'em," he said.

They crowded around him. Ackley lowered his palm. It contained a red cinnamon drop, stained with melted chocolate.

In the silence which followed, the girl's titter sounded like an explosion. The man nudged her as Ackley reached for another piece of candy.

Once more the sergeant drew a red cinnamon drop.

"He switched before he gave you the candy!" he said.

The girl was fingering the chocolates. "I don't think so. This top row seems to have been handled, but the other row doesn't, and it's just in this box. Wait a minute. Here's one—"

Ackley grabbed it and broke it open. He pulled out a small object from the interior, then let out a yell.

"This is one!"

It was a blood-red ruby. Then Ackley cursed again.

"Hell, this is the one I planted there myself!"

And he started breaking open the chocolate creams. His hands became soggy messes, but he found no more rubies.

"Where's Leith?" he asked.

He might as well have asked the wind what had become of the breeze. For Lester Leith, taking advantage of the absence of shadows, had disappeared.

His apartment remained untenanted, save for the undercover man. His garage remained empty. Lester Leith was somewhere in the teeming city, lying low, waiting for his appointment with Mr. Carter Mills.

And Sergeant Ackley sat back in his swivel chair, blamed his subordinates, and continued to curse.

The entire staff at headquarters was munching chocolate creams and waiting.

Lester Leith, in the living room of Mills's suburban house, set up a blowtorch and a crucible, took a package of cornstarch and some powdered alum from his suitcase. Then he took some waterproof cement and sat cross-legged on the floor.

"Unfortunate robbery you had the other day," he said as he poured a small quantity of cornstarch into the crucible.

Mills grunted.

Leith took a vial from his pocket and handed it to Mills. His greedy eyes devoured the luster of the pearls in the vial.

"We can make our fortune out of this," Mills said and glanced back to the crucible.

To his surprise he found himself looking into the business end of an automatic which had appeared in Leith's hand while Mills's attention had been on the pearls.

Leith smiled. "Take it easy, Mills. You're dealing with big stuff now."

"What do you mean?"

"I'm a gangster. I use gangsters' methods. I've got a mob that'll stop at nothing. Griggy the Gat was one of my men."

Beads of perspiration stood out on the jeweler's forehead. He kept his eyes on the gun.

"You see, you made up your mind a long time ago to steal those gems from the rajah," went on Lester Leith, his voice ominously smooth. "So you deliberately arranged for a lot of newspaper publicity about how you carried a million dollars in gems back and forth from your work.

"Naturally I fell for it. I told Griggy the Gat to get into your place, collar you when you came in, and grab the stones. Griggy muffed the job, but mostly because you had it all figured out. You knew a clever yeggman would probably strike just when you entered your place of business in the morning.

"You're smart, Mills, and that's why you always came to work a few minutes before anyone else showed up. You gave a stickup just that opening, hoping he'd fall.

"What happened was just what you hoped for—that the stickup would get killed in a gun battle with the cops.

"Griggy the Gat got the bum breaks, you got the good ones. The bulls looked all over and couldn't find the stones. That was natural—*because they hadn't been in the briefcase in the first place!*

"Then you made a fool move. You were afraid the police would reach the right conclusion when they searched every place they could think of and still didn't find the stones. You wanted to convince them that the gems *had* been stolen. So you started to put some of them in circulation.

"You were clever enough to know that the average person never remembers more than one distinctive feature, or two at the most. You pulled a cap well down on your head and put a patch over one eye. Those two things were obvious.

The people you dealt with saw them, and saw nothing else. But you made a mistake when you had the patch over the left eye on one occasion and over the right on another. Yet you fooled the police."

"What do you want?" asked Mills.

"A cut, of course."

Mills wet his lips. "You can't prove a thing. I'm not going to be held up."

Lester Leith glanced at his watch.

"It may interest you to know," he said, "that the police have at last reached the conclusion they should have reached before. Having decided that the gems were not concealed by Griggy the Gat, and having convinced themselves the gems were not on Griggy at the time of his death, they have concluded you didn't give them to Griggy. Therefore, they have decided you slipped over a fast one. So they took your picture, made a life-size enlargement, put a cap on it and a patch over one eye, and the witnesses have identified it as the man who gave out four of the rubies."

Mills swallowed with difficulty.

Lester Leith holstered his gun.

"After all, it's not my funeral. I've decided to have the gang take you for a little vacation. At a signal from me they'll come in. If you don't kick through with the gems you'll go for a ride."

Mills squirmed. "You said the police—"

Leith glanced at his watch again. "Are on their way. Guess I'd better call in the boys."

Mills choked.

"Last chance." Leith smiled.

Mills shook his head. "No. You're wrong. I haven't got them. I—"

He broke off. From the east sounded the wail of a siren, a wail that grew in volume.

"Save me, the police!" screamed Mills.

Leith struck him across the face.

"Save you, you cheap crook—save myself! Save my boys. They're out there covering me. If the police stop here it'll mean a massacre!"

Mills dived toward a window.

Leith's fist crashed into his jaw and sent him down to the floor.

"You damn fool. Keep away from that window. The police will walk right into an ambush. My choppers will mow them down. You know what that means. When you kill a cop there's always hell to pay."

The siren keened even louder.

"Seems to be right in my garage!" said Mills.

"Then listen for firing," said Leith.

Bang! Bang! Bang! Poppety-pop-pop-pop-bang!

"Riot guns!" yelled Leith.

For a space of seconds the explosions continued, and then silence descended.

Leith sighed. "Well, you've done it. My men have wiped out the cops—it's a massacre. Naturally the bulls will blame you for the job. It's the chair for you—unless—"

"Unless what?"

"Unless I decide to take you into the gang. We can use a good jewel man."

Mills struggled to his hands and knees. "I won't stand for it. I'll stay right here and explain to the officers."

Leith laughed grimly.

"Listen, fat guy," he said. "My men have just mowed down a squad of bluecoats. Think I'm going to get soft over one more murder?"

He took out his automatic and sighted it. His eyes gleamed with the fury popularly supposed to possess a murderer at the moment of the kill.

"No, No! I'll kick through, wait!"

Mills scrambled to his feet, scuttled to the hall, and took a thick cane from the hall tree where it had been hanging in plain sight.

"Here they are," he said, thrusting the cane into Leith's hands. "Come on, quick. I'll throw in with you!"

Lester Leith shook the cane.

"No, no. You can't tell by shaking. It's balanced with sheet lead and stuffed with cotton. The gems are nested in the cotton. You get into it by unscrewing the ferrule."

"All right, Mills," Leith said. "Better go out to your garage and start sweeping up the firecrackers. And you'll find a siren connected so that it would start to wail when a piece of punk burned through a connection, just before the firecrackers went off. I was celebrating the Fourth of July."

Mills tried to speak, but the sounds that came out were not words.

"Good morning," said Lester Leith.

"The—the—police!" stuttered Mills.

"Oh, yes, the police. They are still groping in the dark. I solved the case because the police proved my suspicions by a process of elimination. You see, your inordinate desire for newspaper publicity made me a little suspicious at the first. Then when the police looked *everywhere* that Griggy might have concealed the stones and didn't find a trace, my suspicion became a certainty."

And Lester Leith strolled from the front door with all the ease of a man who is very sure of himself.

Sergeant Ackley was pacing the floor of Leith's apartment when Lester Leith entered.

"Well, well, Sergeant! Waiting for me?"

Sergeant Ackley spoke with the slow articulation of a man who is trying to control his rage.

"Get the stones?" he asked.

Lester Leith raised his eyebrows. "Pardon?"

Sergeant Ackley took a deep breath. "You ditched the shadows yesterday and disappeared!"

Lester Leith lit a cigarette.

"Sit down, Sergeant. You're frightfully fidgety. Overwork, I guess. No, Sergeant, as it happened, your shadows ditched me."

"Well," growled the officer, "either way, you disappeared and didn't come home last night."

Leith's smile became a chuckle. "Purely a private affair, Sergeant."

"Then you called on Mills and set off a bunch of firecrackers."

"Quite right, Sergeant. This is the Fourth of July, you know, according to my special heat-saving calendar. I was celebrating. Mills didn't complain, did he?"

Sergeant Ackley twisted the cigar from the left side of his mouth to the right.

"That," he said, "is the funny part of the whole thing. Mills seems to think there isn't any cause for making a squawk. And I ain't satisfied about that candy yet. There are some things in this caper I've missed. That girl and her boyfriend, for instance—couldn't even hold them, no evidence. Couldn't be they were working for you, Leith, in your pay?"

Lester Leith smiled. "Tut, tut, Sergeant, you *couldn't* have missed anything."

Sergeant Ackley headed for the door.

"Leith, I think you're a crook. Sort of a supercrook, a lucky crook—but a crook. Someday I'm going to get you."

Ackley paused on the threshold. "Next time the instructions will be what they should have been this time, and every time—*tail Leith!*"

And the door slammed.

Lester Leith turned beamingly to his valet, who had been standing by during the interview.

"Scuttle, I feel that a heat-saving calendar isn't as simple as it seemed. Turn on the heat full force, and then see if you can't pick up a new calendar somewhere. I'm going back to November."

"Now that the firecrackers are exploded," said the valet.

Lester Leith smiled again. "Certainly, Scuttle. You wouldn't expect me to carry over a big investment in firecrackers, would you?"

The valet sighed resignedly. "Begging your pardon, sir, I'd expect you to do almost anything—and get away with it sir."

The Vanishing Corpse

THERE was much distinctly feline about the ability of Sidney Zoom to prowl around in dark places. He had a catfooted silence of motion, and his eyes had that peculiar quality of adjustment which enabled him to see in the dark.

More—he loved the mysteries of dark side streets, of deserted whaives.

Micky O'Hara, the officer who had the waterfront beat that embraced Piers 44 to 59, had grown accustomed to the gaunt form that appeared mysteriously from the darkness, strode silently across lighted patches, and disappeared in gloomy blotches of shadow. Always that figure was accompanied by an alert police dog which padded faithfully at the side of his master, ears, eyes and nose keenly aware of the activities of the night.

For Sidney Zoom's yacht was moored at the foot of Pier 47, and dog and master could never sleep without a midnight patrol of the dark places.

Long ago Officer O'Hara had given up trying to chat with the aloof figure. Zoom's strange personality contained a grimness that was a wall of defense to friendly advances. Only his secretary, Vera Thurmond, with her woman's instinct, had learned that back of this wall was a vast yearning, a loneliness of soul which craved companionships the personality repelled.

To the world Sidney Zoom was a mystery, a strange man who came and went, who aided misfortune, yet detested weakness.

On this summer night the darkness had a velvet texture, a warm lure of hinted adventure. Officer O'Hara patrolled his lonely beat with a sense of physical well-being, yet with an inner restlessness.

A hundred yards ahead of him, the darkness of an alley between wharves seemed to move with black life. The officer stopped stock-still. The darkness churned with silent motion.

The officer slipped well toward the walls of the dock buildings and started to walk rapidly, noiselessly.

When he had covered some thirty yards, he saw a stalking figure move out of the patch of darkness. Beside that figure, padding stride for stride, came the form of a tawny police dog, well-muscled, steel-tendoned.

Officer O'Hara's hand came away from his hip. He sighed.

There was no use accosting Sidney Zoom, or giving him a greeting.

The police dog flung his head in a half circle of listening attention and growled. Then, as the warm night breeze carried the scent of Officer O'Hara to the dog's nostrils, the throaty growl subsided, and the dog gave his tail a brief wag.

So much he gave by way of friendly greeting, and no more. The dog reflected the personality of his master.

Sidney Zoom did not even look around, but strode across the lighted sidewalk to the next alley which opened between the rambling buildings, the littered wharves, and vanished, swallowed in the shadows.

Sometimes Officer O'Hara patrolled those wharf alleys. Upon such occasions he took out his electric flashlight and sent the beam cutting through the thick darkness. For it was like the inside of a pocket in those gloomy passageways, at one end of which the lighted street showed as a golden oblong, at the other end of which the lap-lapping of waters gave forth a sound of ceaseless mystery.

But Sidney Zoom made his way through the darkness with sure-footed stealth, a shadow within shadows, a bit of moving darkness against the black blob of night.

Officer O'Hara had come almost even with the alley mouth into which Zoom and his dog had disappeared when he heard a sudden scream, the patter of swift-running feet.

He stepped back, flattened against the wall of one of the rambling structures, reached for his night stick and made sure that his revolver was loose in its holster.

From the mouth of the alley, plunging from the darkness into the light of the street, came a swift figure. It ran with the light agility of a startled deer.

Officer O'Hara jumped forward.

"Halt!" he yelled.

The running man gave one frightened glance, then burst into fresh speed.

O'Hara tried to give chase.

He sighed as he realized the futility of his efforts. Running with a flatfooted stride in which main strength and awkwardness predominated, he was no match for the slender figure that slipped along the pavement like a wild thing.

O'Hara pulled out his blue steel weapon and prepared to fire a shot in the air. If that wasn't sufficient . . .

There was a swirl of motion behind him.

The night gave forth a soft tattoo of beating feet. The police dog went past him like a flash of light.

Officer O'Hara lowered his gun and slowed his speed.

He could hear the pad of cushioned feet on the pavement, claws scraping cement, and then the running figure gave one frantic glance of alarm, one more scream.

The police dog went into the air like a steel spring. The shoulder of the dog crashed against the back of the running figure, and the momentum of that impact sent the runner staggering, off balance.

A stumble, and the man was down.

The dog stood over him, fangs bared, a rumbling growl coming from the throat. Yet his ears were cocked, alert and interested.

There was another rush of motion.

For the second time a sprinting body hurtled past Officer O'Hara. This time it was Sidney Zoom, running easily.

"Watch out! He may have a gun!" panted the officer.

But Sidney Zoom gave the warning no heed.

He sprinted up to the sprawled figure and made a gesture with his hand. The dog, obedient to that gesture, drew back.

"Get up," said Sidney Zoom.

At that moment Officer O'Hara arrived.

"What's—it—all—about?" he asked, panting heroically after his sprint.

But the question was unanswered. The figure rolled to its side, pillowed a head in an arm and started to sob.

"A hell of a guy!" said O'Hara, staring scornfully at the slight form that was a huddle of black on the sidewalk, shaking with sobs. "Get up!"

And he reached a brawny hand to the collar of the coat.

The paunchy weight of the officer, which had hindered him as a runner, gave him the advantage here. As a steel derrick lifts a weight, the strong arm of the policeman hoisted the slender figure up to its feet and to the light.

"B'gosh!" exclaimed the officer as the cap fell off and a shock of coppery hair dropped to the shoulders. "It's a woman—a slip of a girl!"

Sheer surprise held him speechless.

She was dressed in the clothes of a man, just a trifle too large for her. Her eyes were dark with terror. The lips were pale, the cheeks chalky. She was young, and yet there was an air of self-reliance about her, despite the white terror which gripped her.

Officer O'Hara had within him a paternal streak, but the years of pavement pounding as an officer had dulled his sympathies.

"Now then, young lady," he growled, "out with it!"

But the girl shook her head. Despite her fear there was determination in that headshake.

"Who are you?"

Another shake of the head.

"What were you doing here?"

Silence.

"Why did you run?"

More silence.

Officer O'Hara produced his handcuffs. The streetlight glittered from the nickeled steel.

"I'll be putting the bracelets on yez, and callin' the wagon," he said.

This threat had always before been more than sufficient to crash through the silence of any woman. But, in this case, the threat was in vain. The girl stood, slender, silent, uncomplaining. The fear was still in her eyes, but her lips were clamped with decision.

"Perhaps," said Sidney Zoom, "we can go back to the wharf and see what she was doing."

It was the first time he had spoken. His voice held a peculiar timbre, something of the same quality which makes the blood quiver at the sound of a tom-tom beating, or the booming of an African drum as it throbs out of the jungle darkness.

Officer O'Hara put out his big hands, patting the garments of the girl with a practiced hand. She winced at his first touch, then stood still. Nor did she move when the officer gave an explanation and plunged his hand into the inside pocket of the coat. He brought out a pearl-handled revolver, short-barreled, nickeled.

He broke it open.

The brass shells showed as dull circles of coppery color, and two of those shells showed the mark of a firing pin. The other four were unfired.

Officer O'Hara smelled the muzzle of the gun.

"Shot recently—within an hour," he said, and glared accusingly at the girl.

"This," he added, almost regretfully, "is serious."

The girl said nothing.

He snapped one of the handcuffs around her unresisting right wrist, led her back to the wharf from which she had rushed. His flashlight sent a white beam darting among piled boxes, odds and ends of junk, out into the darkness where the bay swallowed the beam of light.

Sidney Zoom scorned such a laborious method of search. He caught the eye of the police dog.

"Find, Rip," he said.

The dog darted on ahead, nose to the rough timbers, giving an audible sniffing as he ran in questing circles. He picked up the trail, followed it, getting off to one side from time to time, only to swing back.

The girl hung back until the steel bit into her wrist.

Officer O'Hara raised his flashlight. The dog gave a single swift bark, then remained poised, forepaws spread apart, eyes glittering greenly in the light that was reflected from the flashlight.

Between those forepaws was a little black object, a hand purse of metal mesh, lacquered black.

Officer Hara stooped and reached.

The dog's fangs glittered in the light as he made a snapping charge. Zoom snapped a command. The dog drew back, wagged his tail and sat down.

O'Hara picked up the bag.

"This yours?" he asked the girl.

She made no answer.

The officer opened the bag. He handed his flashlight to Sidney Zoom, who played the light beam upon the interior of the bag.

There was a powder puff, a handkerchief, a metal-cased lipstick, and a pasteboard cartridge box upon which was a green label bearing the name of a well-known manufacturer of ammunition.

The officer took the box from the purse. It was heavy. He shook it, then pulled back the cover.

It was about half filled with cartridges. The rest was wadded with cotton. The officer pulled back that cotton, then gasped. His sucked-in breath was an exclamation. His eyes bulged with sheer surprise.

For the beam of the flashlight seemed to have been magnified a thousandfold and then split up into coruscating beams of purple-white fire that darted about like some imprisoned display of northern lights.

"A diamond!" he exclaimed.

The stone was white, polished, filled with cold fire, and it was so large that it might well have caused the officer to exclaim.

He turned accusingly to the girl.

She shrugged her shoulders.

"The Diamond of Death," she said, casually, as one might mention the title of a book, and then she became silent once more.

Special Detective Sam Frankly arrived on the scene

within fifteen minutes of the time Officer O'Hara placed a call from the police box. He inspected the wharf, the purse, the diamond and the prisoner.

Zoom's story was simple. He had seen the figure jump from the dark shadows and throw something in the direction of the water. That something had thudded to the planks of the wharf floor. Then the figure had sprinted past him.

Knowing that Officer O'Hara was coming along the street, and thinking the running figure would plump directly into his arms, Sidney Zoom had not given chase at first, nor had he released his police dog. It was only when he saw that the runner had turned the other way, that O'Hara was getting ready to shoot, that he had allowed the dog to sprint and capture the fugitive. Then Zoom had run swiftly after the dog to be where he could control him. During all of that time he had thought the fugitive was a man.

The detective listened with scowling perplexity.

The girl would say absolutely nothing. She had apparently tried to throw the purse with the cartridge box and the diamond into the black waters of the bay. There it would have splashed from sight and never been recovered. She had failed by a matter of inches. The black mesh bag had been within a foot and a half of the water when the dog had found it.

The girl refused to give her name, her address, or to account for her presence. Detective Frankly put her into his car and took her to headquarters. He was closely followed by Sidney Zoom, who was on terms of intimacy with most of the police department heads.

An examination by the matron revealed that the girl had retained her feminine underwear under her masculine disguise. The underwear had been tailored. Police had ascertained the name of the maker by a sewed-in label, had routed him out of bed and learned that the girl was probably Miss

Mildred Kroom, a niece of Harrison Stanwood, who was an eccentric collector, residing in the exclusive district in the west end.

Since this was kept from the girl, she felt certain that her incognito had been maintained, and she still kept her silence.

Zoom had solved several mysteries for the police. He was friendly with the executive heads, and he knew just how far a civilian could, and could not, go in connection with police activities.

Hence Lieutenant Sylvester decided to ride out to Stanwood's house with Zoom in Zoom's car and let the squad of detectives go in the police car.

They arrived at about the same time.

The men were taking no chances. Two of them darted through the shadows to the back of the house before the other two detectives thumped up on the front porch and pressed the bell button.

The interior of the house jangled with the summons of the bell for many minutes before there was an answering stir of sound from an upper floor. Then they heard the shuffle of slippered feet on the stairs, and a Japanese servant attired in silken bathrobe and with sleep-swollen eyes demanded to know who was ringing the bell.

Satisfied that it was the police, he opened the door and the men walked into a reception hall and through it into a library.

Lieutenant Sylvester took charge of the questioning.

"Mildred Kroom lives here?"

"Yes-s-s-s," said the Japanese.

"Tell her we want to talk with her."

"She is-s-s asleep."

"All right. We'll go up. Show us her room."

The servant hesitated for a fraction of a second, then shrugged his shoulders. He went up the stairs. Two of the men followed him.

There could be heard the sound of a muffled knocking, twice repeated, then the rattle of a doorknob. Voices rumbled in conversation. Then there were feet on the stairs once more, followed by a shuffle of slippers and a voice that hysterically rattled excited comment.

The detectives came into the room.

With them was a man in bathrobe and pajamas whose tousled hair gave him a look of wild excitement. He did not need to be questioned. Words flowed from his lips with the explosive rapidity of bullets from a machine gun.

During the few seconds that sufficed for him to enter the library and be seated, Sidney Zoom was able to get a more or less complete history of the man.

His name was Charles Wetler. He was a secretary to Harrison Stanwood. He said the girl, Mildred Kroom, a niece, rather an erratic, impulsive girl who had been expelled from college, had come to assist her uncle in research work and had been the cause of considerable anxiety. She had speculated on the stock market and lost heavily. Yet she was the only kin of Harrison Stanwood, and he was fond of her.

Lieutenant Sylvester advised Zoom of what had been discovered from a hasty search of the girl's bedchamber. The bed had not been slept in. Her clothes were scattered about. Bureau drawers had been hurriedly ransacked. The girl was missing. It became more apparent than ever that the girl who had made such a mysterious appearance within the dark alley between the wharves was Mildred Kroom, but what she was doing there was an unanswered question.

The officers made a hasty check of the other occupants of the house. There were the Japanese servant, Hashinto Shinahara, an assistant, Oscar Rabb, and Philip Buntler, an old friend. Harrison Stanwood was a collector of rare gems, paintings and curios. He wrote articles from time to time. The articles were authoritative and compiled after the most exhaustive research.

The officer ordered the household to be aroused.

Phil Buntler was fully clothed. His drab eyes were preoccupied with thought, but there was no trace of sleep in them. He said he had been sitting up, reading an interesting work on rare pottery.

His mind seemed still wrapped in the contents of the book. He frowned when he learned of the reason for his being summoned into the drawing room. His comment on the wild pranks of the present generation was scathing, unsympathetic.

Oscar Rabb was a young man, nervously alert, attentive, but with a washed-out personality. He seemed a yes man who would agree to anything.

The Japanese servant showed his teeth through lips that smiled, and regarded the visitors through black eyes that were unsmiling.

Harrison Stanwood did not answer the knocks on his bedroom door. The Japanese servant made the report. The officers went up to investigate. They found the bedroom empty, nor were there any signs that it had been occupied that evening.

Questioning elicited the fact that Stanwood sometimes worked late in his study, poring over books and tabulating facts. The study was on the ground floor, but a short distance from the library.

The men moved toward it in a knot. It seemed that some unspoken thought actuated them with a common purpose, gave to their quest some pall of impending disaster.

It was Charles Wetler, walking rapidly in advance, with nervous, jerky strides, who tried the study door. It was locked.

"Oh, Mr. Stanwood!" he called.

Silence.

"Got an extra key?" asked Lieutenant Sylvester.

The men stared at each other vacantly.

"Can do," said the Japanese, producing a key from his pocket.

The police officer looked at him in suspicious appraisal for a moment, then fitted the key to the lock. The bolt clicked. They crowded together, each one anxious to peer over the threshold, then they fell back.

The room showed that there had been considerable commotion in it. There were books on the floor, drawers had been pulled from tables. The safe was open and the papers and contents had been thrown on the floor. There was a dark red pool of a gruesome character in the center of the table.

It reflected the lights as in a dulled, red mirror.

There was no sign of Harrison Stanwood.

Phil Buntler grunted, staring with his preoccupied eyes at the red blotch on the table.

"Murder," he said.

Lieutenant Sylvester turned to the knot of men.

"Get out," he snapped, "and stay out. We'll send for you as we want you. Joe, you and Jerry see that these men don't separate. Take them in the library and keep 'em there.

"Pete, you and Tom better come in and help me check things over."

Sidney Zoom strode back to the library.

He paced the floor with long, nervous strides. From time to time he lit a cigarette, inhaled fiercely. His head was thrust forward, his eyes gleamingly alert. They were the seeing eyes of a hawk, black pinpoints in the center of twin chunks of cold ice. Unwinking, he stared at the floor as he paced the room.

The others huddled into a group, seemingly wishing the protection of human companionship to guard them against the black mystery of the house. From time to time they talked in low, cautious tones. The detectives listened attentively to every word and that air of concentrated listening had its effect. Conversation died to a dribble, then faded away entirely.

A door slammed.

Steps pounded down the corridor.

Lieutenant Sylvester stared grimly into the room. His eyes were dark and smoldering. He spoke savagely.

"A nice mess," he said. "There's a typewritten note in that room threatening Stanwood with abduction if he doesn't pay twenty thousand dollars. The note claims he will be drugged and 'removed.'

"And there's the will, lying right out on top where we'd be sure to see it. That will leaves half of the fortune to Mildred Kroom. The other half goes to his employees with a share to his dear friend, Philip Buntler.

"That makes everyone here a possible beneficiary and gives everyone a possible motive. What do you say to that, eh?"

The men looked at each other, each trying to read the other's expression.

"Murdered!" blurted Oscar Rabb.

"They can't prove a murder unless they find the body," said Phil Buntler, speaking almost dreamily. "They've got to find a *corpus delicti*."

Lieutenant Sylvester crossed the room, thrust his face close to the scientist and snarled, "Is *that* so! You seem to have been reading up on the law of murders!"

But Buntler was unconcerned. He nodded casually.

"Happened to read a detective story a few days ago that mentioned the point. I asked a lawyer friend about it, just out of curiosity. He said it was so. No corpse, no murder, no murder, no conviction. That's the law."

Lieutenant Sylvester retained his menacing manner.

"Well, my friend, that crack is quite likely to send you to the chair."

Buntler wrinkled his eyebrows. His washed-out eyes seemed to widen and gain something of a sparkle.

"Me?"

The officer's answer was like the crack of a whiplash.

"Yes, you!"

The scientist inquired in a mild tone, as though the accusation failed to move him, "Have you, then, found the body?"

"No!" snapped the officer. "I presume you, as a scientist, know of several ways a body could be disintegrated and destroyed!"

Buntler puckered his forehead in thought.

"Only two," he said, then added, as an afterthought, "that would be practical."

Sylvester shook his head.

"No," he said. "If you'd done it you'd have been smooth enough to keep from making incriminating statements."

His knuckles rubbed against each other as he seesawed his clenched hands back and forth. "Look here," he said, "any of you ever hear of a big diamond that Stanwood had? A stone that might be called the Diamond of Death?"

Phil Buntler nodded, a nod of precise affirmation.

"Now that I think of the matter," he said, "I am convinced that you are referring to the rather large diamond that came from one of the tombs which I uncovered in the Amazon district.

"These tombs dated back hundreds of years to a lost race

that seemed to have vanished from the earth. The tombs were overgrown with jungle growth and were discovered quite by accident. They contained the usual curse to prevent ghouls from disturbing the remains. I gave the diamond to my friend, Harrison. Doubtless it would be referred to by some of the more tragic-minded as the Diamond of Death."

The Japanese servant bowed.

"Car gone, sir," he said.

"Whose car?"

"Boss man's car, sir."

"A sedan, a big Packard," said Wetler. "It's colored a light blue."

The Japanese nodded.

"Probably taken by the girl," observed one of the officers.

The Japanese shook his head.

"No, sir. Girl take her car. Ford car."

Sylvester's forehead creased into a dark frown.

"How do you know?"

The Japanese smirked.

"Car gone, girl gone. Her car. She must have take, sir."

But there was a subtle atmosphere of insincerity about the man that caused the officer to glower at him and roar: "You *know* she took her car! How do you know it?"

The Japanese smirked again.

"Car gone," he said, and a mask of Oriental impassivity settled upon his countenance.

The detectives searched the premises, questioned the men individually, and admitted themselves baffled. It was three o'clock in the morning by the time they decided to concentrate on the girl who was held at headquarters.

Lieutenant Sylvester returned to his office, ordered the girl brought in for questioning. And Sidney Zoom, because he had been a witness to the girl's flight, was allowed to be present.

But that questioning was as futile as had been the previous questions. The girl simply sat mute.

The officer raved, cajoled, threatened. The girl's lips were sealed. She stared straight ahead, eyes expressionless.

The telephone rang.

Lieutenant Sylvester frowned at the instrument, disdaining to answer it. He was concentrating on the task of getting the truth from the lips of the silent girl.

There was an apologetic knock at the door. An officer thrust his head into the room.

"Beg pardon, Lieutenant, but there's a man on the line in connection with this Stanwood affair. It's important."

Lieutenant Sylvester grabbed at the telephone, scooped the receiver to his ear.

"Okay, this is Lieutenant Sylvester speaking. Yeah . . . What? . . . You sure? . . . Where are you now? . . . You know him, eh? . . . You wait there. I'll be there in seven minutes."

He slammed the receiver back on the hook and motioned to an officer to remove the girl from the room. Then he turned to Sidney Zoom.

"Come on, Zoom. Your car's outside and all ready to go. I want you to drive me out to the yacht basin. Your yacht's located out there and you know the country. There's a yachtsman just came in from a long trip, friend of Stanwood's. He says the Stanwood sedan is parked against the side of a wharf with the lights on and old Stanwood is dead inside the car.

"He says there's a dagger in his chest and that the car doors are locked. Funny business. Says there can't be any mistake. He knows Stanwood well, been cruising with him several times."

Zoom was on his feet, a hand on the doorknob.

"Who is the yachtsman?" he asked.

"Chap by the name of Bowditch."

Zoom nodded approvingly.

"I know him well, a conservative man and a good sailor."

They went down the stairs, out into the night that was just commencing to crispen with the tang of early morning. Zoom snapped his roadster into speed. They tore through the deserted streets, flashed past intersections and whizzed into the vicinity of the waterfront.

"A telephone in the Bayside Yacht Club House," said Lieutenant Sylvester. "Know where it is?"

Zoom nodded, pushed down the throttle, swung the car, slammed on the brakes, rounded the corner of an alleyway between two of the wharves, and skidded to a stop where an office-like structure bordered the dark waters of the bay.

The east was just commencing to show streaks of light.

A man came running out to meet the car.

"It's down here a couple of blocks, parked directly in front of where I dock my yacht."

He caught Zoom's eye, started, then nodded.

"Zoom! This is indeed a pleasure. How are you?"

Zoom shook hands and introduced Bowditch to the lieutenant.

"Better hop on the running board," said Sylvester. "This is important."

The man jumped on the running board. Sidney Zoom whirled the car, backed it, cut loose the motor in low gear, and the machine snorted forward like a frisky colt.

They went a block, turned down a little jog in a street, and came to a place where a parked sedan showed a glowing light from the dome globe.

"He's in there. It's ghastly."

Sylvester nodded absent-mindedly. Spectacles that were ghastly meant but little to him. He had seen too many.

"Anybody else see it?" asked Sylvester.

"Yes. There were two of my crew. They were with me

when I came up. I sent them back to the boat, because I was afraid there were rough characters around, and I had some rather valuable things on the yacht."

Sylvester snorted.

"Rough characters is right!" he said.

Zoom drew his car up in behind the parked sedan.

"You'll see it lying there on the floor, the face turned up toward the light. There's a dagger in the breast, right here."

And Bowditch indicated the right lapel of his coat.

Lieutenant Sylvester jumped from the car, lit upon the pavement with eager feet while the others were getting out, and ran to the sedan. He pressed his face against the windows, then jerked futilely at the door.

"It's locked!" said Bowditch. "I tried 'em all."

But Lieutenant Sylvester motioned them back with a fierce gesture.

"Keep away! Don't touch the handles of those doors. I'll be wanting fingerprints. He's been taken out."

"What!" Bowditch yelled incredulously.

Then he craned his neck forward, holding his hands behind him, careful not to touch the handles of the doors. Back of him, several inches taller, Zoom peered over his shoulder.

The sedan was empty.

The dome light showed the interior in a sickly light that was turning wan and yellow now that dawn was in the air. There was a red pool on the carpet in the rear of the sedan, and that was all.

"Sure he was in there?" asked Sylvester skeptically.

"Absolutely certain. I've had him out on my yacht often enough. I should know him when I see him. We've had interests in common. Once we purchased a collection together.

"Outside of Phil Buntler, I'm about the only close friend he has in the world. I saw him plain, I tell you. And my two men recognized him as the one who had been on cruises with us. He was lying on his back, his face tilted back. It was catching the full rays of the dome light. You couldn't mistake the face. It was Harrison Stanwood all right."

Lieutenant Sylvester nodded.

"Okay. You stick by that story and I'll sure give someone a fry. That establishes the *corpus delicti*. You're sure about the dagger?"

"Absolutely certain."

"And that he was dead?"

"Ugh, I should say so. His face was all gray and his eyes were like glass. They looked awful! Awful!"

The officer nodded grimly.

"Okay. You two stay here. I'm getting down some fingerprint experts. Then I'm going to get rough with somebody."

The police went through their routine. The car was gone over for fingerprints. The locks were removed from the doors. The red pool was tested to make certain that it was human blood.

The fingerprints found on the door handles were those of Frank Bowditch, the yachtsman. There were no other prints save such prints as were old and had been made by Harrison Stanwood himself.

It was Stanwood's car, beyond a doubt. And the man who locked those doors upon the corpse had been careful to remove all fingerprints—unless that man had been Bowditch.

But what happened to the body after it had been found in the parked car? Why was it that the girl's coat pocket held a thirty-eight-caliber revolver with two discharged shells, while Stanwood seemed to have been done to death with a dagger?

Sidney Zoom retired to his own yacht and apparently lost interest in the case. But he scanned the newspapers and from time to time rang up friends in the police department.

The police had found a bullet embedded in the wall at

Stanwood's house. That bullet had been fired from the weapon found in the girl's pocket. That much the experts agreed upon with absolute certainty. But the girl refused to talk. Her silence continued in spite of all sorts of threats. On the other hand, she employed no attorney and seemed content to remain in jail pending further investigation by the police.

Matters continued at that deadlock for an even week. Then the body of Harrison Stanwood was discovered in its final resting place.

This time there was no question of a corpse being spirited away from under the noses of the police.

Children playing in a rubbish heap had noticed the foot of a man sticking out from under some cans. They had summoned parents. The parents had summoned the police.

The body was decomposed, but identification was positive.

There was a bullet in the left shoulder. That bullet, also, had come from the weapon which had been found in the girl's pocket. There was a dagger wound in the left side of the chest, and that dagger wound had undoubtedly resulted in death. The blade had penetrated the heart.

Sidney Zoom read of the gruesome find and nodded his head. So might a man nod who had predicted a certain event, and that event had duly come to pass.

Zoom rang up Lieutenant Sylvester.

"The Kroom girl will talk now. I'll be interested to know what she says," he said.

The voice which rasped over the wire at him was keen with impatience.

"How do you know she'd talk now?"

"I just guessed she would."

"Well, you're a good guesser. She's told her story and hired a lawyer. Whether we can keep her or not I don't know."

"What was her story?"

"Better come up to headquarters. There are a couple of questions I want to ask you. You may turn out to be the main witness of the prosecution against the girl."

Sidney Zoom smiled grimly.

"I *may*," he admitted, and hung up the reciever.

There had, for years, been a friendship between Sidney Zoom and Captain Mahoney of the police force. The two men held each other in mutual respect, which is the basis of all lasting friendship.

Zoom was surprised to find that Captain Mahoney was awaiting him at headquarters when he came to answer Lieutenant Sylvester's questions.

Mahoney was a small man with a large mind. He had a voice which was rarely raised above a conversational tone, and he did not usually concern himself greatly over individual cases, but gave his attention to matters of policy.

Now he was smoking a long perfecto with those meditative puffs which denote the thinker. He shook hands.

"Sit down, Sidney. I want to talk with you."

Zoom sat down and crossed his long legs.

"The girl's acting funny. She's acted funny all the way through," said the police captain.

Zoom nodded.

"She never made any statement or any defense until the body was found and she knew just where that bullet from her gun was located. Then she got an attorney.

"Here's her story—now that she's consulted with her lawyer. How much of it is hers and how much of it is his I don't know.

"She claims she had been out on a party that had quite a bit of action and some gin, that she came home and went to see her uncle, that there was a light in his study and the door was unlocked. She walked in and found the room in confusion, very much as we found it.

"She says she was panicky and that she went out and locked the door and ran to her room. She always had the revolver in her dresser drawer, and something made her look for it. She found it in place, but detected an odor of burned powder, so she broke it open and found two shots had been fired.

"Then she happened to look in her jewel case and found the big diamond that she calls the Diamond of Death. It seems she'd given it that tag in talking with her uncle. The girl's superstitious, or claims she is, or her lawyer claims it for her. It'll sound all the same to a jury.

"She figured that her uncle had been murdered and that someone intended to blame the crime on her. So she started looking for anything else that might have been planted in her room.

"She turned everything upside down in a hurried search, then put the incriminating articles in a metal mesh bag and started for the waterfront to throw them in the bay. She said she figured that she might be watched, and that no matter where she concealed the things they'd be found. But if she pitched them in the bay it would be impossible to find them.

"Now here's the case we've got against her. The diamond belonged to the dead man. The bullet from her revolver was found in his body, although not in a position that would prove fatal. Her Ford car was found parked within two blocks of where you found her when she was trying to dispose of the stuff.

"The sedan belonging to Harrison Stanwood was found within half a dozen blocks of where her Ford was parked. That car held the body. It was locked in the car and the lights were on. Later on the body disappeared.

"But there are holes in the case. The girl has played a game that's almost sure to win. She's kept her mouth shut until she's found out everything that we have. Then, when she knows our complete case, she starts talking and gets a lawyer to coach her.

"Now there's a lot of public sentiment against this girl. The circumstantial evidence against her points to cold-blooded murder. But we can't afford to guess wrong. We can't afford to have a case of this sort result in an acquittal. If she's innocent, we've got to know it now."

Captain Mahoney peered shrewdly at Sidney Zoom.

Zoom lit a cigarette, took a deep drag, snapped the match out with an impatient gesture of the wrist and nodded.

"She is," he said.

"Is what?"

"Innocent."

Sylvester snorted.

"You talk like a fish!"

"Shut up, Sylvester," said Captain Mahoney.

The two officers looked at Zoom. Sylvester's stare was moodily hostile. Captain Mahoney's glance was that of one who patiently waits.

Sidney Zoom broke the silence at length.

"Was there, perhaps, a cut in the right-hand side of Stanwood's coat when you found the corpse?"

Captain Mahoney's face did not change expression, but Sylvester's face twisted in surprise.

"Yes," said Sylvester.

Zoom pursed his lips thoughtfully and regarded the smoldering tip of his cigarette with judicial deliberation.

"Well?" said Captain Mahoney.

Sidney Zoom's lips twisted in the ghost of a smile.

"You won't believe what I'm going to tell you," he said.

"Go ahead," invited the captain.

Sidney Zoom took a deep inhalation, sucking in the smoke from his cigarette, exhaling it through his nostrils.

"Harrison Stanwood's body wasn't in the sedan when Bow-ditch put in the telephone call," he said.

Sylvester laughed grimly.

"Bowditch was lying, eh? You want to involve him, huh?"

Zoom's smile was paternally patient.

"No. Bowditch thought he saw a body. He didn't."

"What *did* he see, Sidney?" asked Captain Mahoney.

"A wax dummy."

"A what?"

"A wax dummy. The man who committed that murder wanted to make certain it would be blamed on the girl. If there was going to be any hitch in the thing he didn't want to become involved himself.

"He'd handled it all the way through so he could either go ahead with the murder or else quit. If the girl was going to get the blame, he'd go ahead. Otherwise, he'd quit. He knew enough law to know the police needed a *corpus delicti* in order to convict the girl. In this case it meant a corpse.

"Now here's my theory of the case.

"The man who wanted to eliminate Stanwood sneaked up on him, held ether or chloroform to his nostrils, then removed him from the house. Before he did that, he inflicted a superficial wound with the girl's gun, and fired one shot into the woodwork of the study. Then he planted clues in the girl's room.

"The girl suspected something and tried to remove those clues. She was caught. Unwittingly, I helped the real criminal by assisting in retrieving the clues the girl was trying to get rid of.

"But the murderer was playing safe. He had a wax dummy to be used as a corpse. He planted it where it would be seen and identified. After it had been identified as a corpse, he removed it.

"Then he waited. If anyone had suspected him, or if the girl had been able to prove a good alibi, he'd have simply released Stanwood. And Stanwood wouldn't have known but what the real criminal was his rescuer.

"As I reconstruct the crime, the man overpowered Stanwood, kept him unconscious, and kept him under the influence of drugs until he was certain the crime would be blamed on the girl. If he'd been suspected, he'd have let Stanwood regain consciousness, then rescued him from his prison and taken a lot of credit for solving the mystery.

"That's why the coat was cut on the right side. The way the figure was jammed into the sedan left the right side uppermost. The man who pulled the job wanted to make sure the knife would show, so he stuck it into the upper side."

Captain Mahoney shook his head.

"No, Zoom, I'm afraid that's too improbable."

Sylvester laughed aloud.

"I've heard some wild ones in my time," he said. "But that's the wildest I ever did hear."

Sidney Zoom smoked complacently in calm silence.

After a few moments Captain Mahoney shot a series of swift questions at him.

"What made you think of this solution, Sidney?"

"Several things. A real corpse couldn't have been juggled around so handily. It's more than a coincidence that the dummy corpse was parked where about the only man who could positively identify it would see it."

"How do you figure this drugging stuff?"

"Easy. The man drugged Stanwood. He wanted to lay the foundation for an abduction, so he wrote a note and left it in plain sight, stating that Stanwood would be drugged and kidnaped unless he paid some blackmail money."

"Do you know who this man was?"

"No."

"Have you any suspicions?"

"Only generally."

"He could have been any one of the men who lived in the house and who were trusted by Stanwood?"

"Yes."

"Can you prove the guilt of that man, if your theory is correct?"

Zoom shrugged his shoulders.

"Only by getting him to commit another murder."

"Who would he murder?"

"Me."

"You!"

"Not exactly. He used one dummy to perpetrate his crime. I'd use another to trap him."

"You'd be in some personal danger?"

"Perhaps."

"You think you could solve the crime?"

"Yes."

"What would you want?"

"A brown candle and a microscope," said Zoom, "also to be ensconced in Stanwood's house as a scientific detective employed by the police to clear up the affair."

Sylvester's hearty laugh boomed heavily.

"Of all the damn fool theories!" he roared. "And you want a candle and a microscope. By Gad, Zoom, you're good. You've got so romantic that your brain's addled. Trying to protect a damned little two-timing, gun-toting, man-killing tart that had—"

Captain Mahoney raised his hand.

"Lieutenant," he said, "please see that Sidney Zoom has everything he wants to clear up this crime."

He bowed at Zoom and walked casually from the room.

Sylvester's laugh strangled in his throat.

"Hell!" he said.

Sidney Zoom was duly ensconced as a scientific detective working on the Stanwood murder case. He was given a room in the house of the murdered man and puttered about the corridors with tape measure and magnifying glass. Once or twice he swept up bits of dust and ostentatiously examined them through the binocular microscope which had been given him by the police department.

The occupants of the house watched him with varying expressions.

Charles Wetler, the secretary, was nervously alert to every single move. The Japanese servant, Hashinto Shinahara, was fawningly deferential. Yet, back of all that deference, there was a subtle impression of inward amusement.

Oscar Rabb was anxious to curry favor with the grim-visaged detective. Phil Buntler walked about as one in a dream, his eyes fixed upon space, his head bowed. He was vastly preoccupied, yet occasionally his eyes lost their dreamy abstraction and gazed at Sidney Zoom with pinpointed intensity.

Sidney Zoom worked all one afternoon. Then he retired to his bedroom. That room was at the end of the corridor, off by itself.

He read a book, consulting his watch from time to time. One by one, he could hear the other members of the household ascending stairs, retiring to their rooms.

Zoom waited.

At precisely thirteen minutes to one o'clock in the morning, Zoom opened the door of his room, took out a knife and the brown candle. He shaved the candle and let the shavings drop to the waxed floor of the corridor. He walked the full length of the corridor, sprinkling the wax shavings.

Then he returned to his room and picked up a heavy revolver.

He turned out the light and opened the window.

He pointed the revolver through the open window and fired three times, at intervals. The reports split the nocturnal silence with a roar.

Then Sidney Zoom stretched himself upon the floor, sprawled out, arms and legs extended, placed the revolver upon the floor and closed his eyes.

There were frantic steps in the corridor, voices that were raised in excited comment, a knock upon the door.

He had locked the door, and, when a hand tried the knob and found it locked, Sidney Zoom smiled to himself in the darkness of the room.

There was a hammering on the panels, no mere knock this time, then the sound of a weight thudding against the door.

Zoom realized that the entire household had now assembled.

Finally the combined weight of the hurtling bodies crashed the door open. Light from the corridor streamed in upon the form of Sidney Zoom.

"Murdered," said a cool voice which Zoom recognized as belonging to Phil Buntler.

"Suicide—by Jove!" said Charles Wetler.

"Oh, isn't it horrible!" muttered Oscar Rabb.

Hashinto Shinahara said nothing, but moved forward with catlike quickness and extended a hand.

Sidney Zoom sat up and grinned into the startled faces of his audience.

"Just a little test I had arranged for you boys," he said.

They recoiled.

"Well, it's a rotten test!" snapped Wetler irritably.

Oscar Rabb fidgeted. "I shall be unable to sleep," he said.

Hashinto Shinahara grinned until his white teeth showed in a gleaming circle.

"Very smart!" he exclaimed.

Phil Buntler stared moodily downward at the floor, then

said, "Rather clever. I am glad to be of any assistance, Mr. Zoom. Undoubtedly, wakening persons in the middle of the night, letting them discover what they think is the body of a murdered man, and watching their reactions, is a valuable psychological test.

"If any of us, for instance, had been implicated in the murder of my dear friend, Harrison Stanwood, I have no doubt that a trained psychologist would have detected something in the manner or appearance of us as we burst into the room which would have been a betrayal of guilt."

And he beamed about him at the puzzled faces of the others.

"And you are a trained psychologist, Mr. Zoom?"

And Sidney Zoom, suddenly hard-eyed, nodded curtly.

"I am," he admitted, "and I shall now have to ask that you retire to your rooms, gentlemen."

They retired, muttering.

Zoom stretched himself in an easy chair, picked up his book, lit a cigarette, and smoked as placidly as though nothing out of the ordinary had happened.

When an hour had passed, he took his microscope, a few glass slides and some matches, and started on a tour of the house.

He first came to the bedroom of Phil Buntler. He tapped on the door, heard a swift rustle of motion from the room, the creaking of a bed, and then slippered feet on the floor.

Buntler's eyes stared at Zoom.

"You again, eh? You seem determined we shan't sleep!"

Zoom nodded. "I'm sorry. But this is important. I'll have the murderer by morning. In the meantime I'm afraid I'll have to inconvenience you for a few moments."

He stalked into the room and sat down, depositing the microscope on the table.

"Would you mind removing your slippers and getting back into bed?" he asked.

Buntler kicked his slippers off and returned to the covers.

"I confess," he said sarcastically, "that I am unable to follow your reasoning."

Zoom nodded casually.

"I had hardly expected that you would be able to," he commented, and picked up a pair of shoes as well as the slippers.

He took out a long-bladed knife and started scraping both shoes and slippers, digging carefully into every corner and crease of leather and sole, letting the scrapings drop on a plate of glass. When he had collected them, he scooped them onto a small glass slide and put them under the microscope.

Buntler watched him with interest.

"Humph," said Zoom at length, puzzled.

"What is it?" asked Buntler, interested.

"Something funny on your shoes," remarked Zoom.

Buntler's bare feet hit the floor. "Mind if I look?" he asked.

Zoom drew back from the microscope.

Buntler peered through the lenses. "Little grains of dirt, and . . . oh, yes—you mean those flat translucent flakes?"

"Yes."

"Hmmmm," muttered Buntler to himself.

At length he raised his head and shrugged his shoulders.

"What's it all about?" he asked.

Zoom pulled the slide from the microscope and struck a match. He held the glass slide over the flame of the match for several seconds. Then he took a handkerchief and wiped the black from the places where the flame had touched, and thrust the slide under the microscope again.

He peered at it, then chuckled.

"Look," he said.

Buntler looked.

"It's melted," he observed. "Evidently a colored paraffin or wax."

Zoom nodded, took a vial from his pocket and in it deposited the contents of the slide.

"Please remain in your room," he said, and stalked into the hall.

He went at once to the room of Oscar Rabb and knocked at the door.

Rabb was not in bed, but was seated in a rocking chair. Zoom heard him get up, heard the click of the bolt. The door opened a crack.

Rabb was staring, white-faced, a magazine in his hand.

"You again!" he said.

"Yes," said Zoom, and entered the room.

Once more he took out his knife, scraped off the soles of slippers and shoes, put the scrapings together upon the glass slide. Once more he called for the occupant of the room to peer through the microscope lenses at the strange flakes of translucent material which were mixed in with the dirt particles.

Rabb was as puzzled over their nature as Buntler had been until Zoom applied the flame of the match and invited Rabb to again look through the lenses.

"Humph!" said Rabb, "looks like some wax from a candle!"

Zoom nodded, dumped the scrapings into a glass vial, picked up the microscope and cautioned Rabb to remain in his room.

He next entered Wetler's room and went through the same procedure.

Wetler had been lying on the bed. At Zoom's first knock there had been a gentle snore audible through the panels of the door. It had taken three knocks to get Wetler up.

Wetler surveyed the flakes which Zoom found in the scrapings and shrugged his shoulders. After the flakes were heated he examined them again.

"They've melted!" he exclaimed, when he had his eyes glued to the microscope.

"Yes," said Zoom, "they've melted."

Wetler muttered a puzzled exclamation. His forehead was creased in thought.

"What," he asked, "could they possibly be?"

Sidney Zoom dumped the scrapings into a numbered glass vial.

"I don't know. I'll have to make further tests," he said. "Please remain in your room."

And he went into the corridor, walked down the stairs, and tapped on the door of Hashinto Shinahara's room.

The Japanese servant was at the door in a single spring, as lithe as a cat. He flung open the door, stood in the entrance half crouched, his eyes narrowed to gleaming slits, his hands curved like talons.

Sidney Zoom explained his errand.

The face of the Japanese wreathed itself in smiles. "Come in, come in," he said.

Sidney Zoom made the same tests, secured the same flake-like substances, let the servant see them both before and after he had applied the match.

But Hashinto Shinahara volunteered no statement of any sort. He sucked in his breath once, the sound plainly audible as the air hissed past his teeth. But he continued to smile with his lips. His eyes were utterly inscrutable.

Sidney Zoom deposited the scrapings in a glass vial, screwed on the cap, and ordered the Japanese to remain in his room.

Then he padded down the corridor to the telephone.

It was precisely two o'clock, and he had left instructions

for Lieutenant Sylvester to await a call from him at precisely
two o'clock.

Zoom made no effort to lower his voice. "I'm on the trail
of something hot in that Stanwood case, Lieutenant," he
said.

There was a moment of silence, then a question rasped
over the wire.

Zoom answered it at length.

"In the first place," he said, "the basic theory of the department has been wrong. The theory has been that the
niece left the will out in plain sight because she was anxious
it be discovered, since it gave her half of the property.

"As a matter of fact, since the niece was the only kin, she
would have taken it *all* if it hadn't been for the will. Therefore, it would have been to her interests to have destroyed
the will.

"There's another thing that must be remembered. The
body of Harrison Stanwood was found in a car by a yachtsman who was one of the few intimate friends Stanwood had.
That car was parked where the yachtsman was bound to notice it when he returned from his cruise. And the state of the
tide governed the time of his return, so that one who knew
the habits of yachtsmen could have come pretty close to determining just when Bowditch would have been passing the
sedan.

"Now notice that the body was lying in a position to make
it readily identified. That the knife was in the right side.
That, when Bowditch went to telephone the police, the body
was removed. That, when the body was discovered, there was
a slit in the coat on the right side, as though a knife had been
plunged in there, but there was no corresponding mark on
the corpse.

"Notice, also, that the girl was locked up while the body
was removed. It was physically impossible for her to have

moved that body. She was in jail. Notice, also, that the doors of the sedan were locked and that the dome light was on, and that the body was placed in such a position the rays of the dome light fell upon the face.

"Those things are the determining circumstances in the solution I have worked out. But a certain discovery I have made has clinched the case.

"I'm going to go to the place where the body was discovered, the rubbish heap where you finally found the body. I think I can show you something interesting. I'll go there at once. It's nearer here than it is headquarters, so I'll be waiting for you there. I'll have my car parked against the curb and leave the dome light on so you can recognize me. Good-by."

And Sidney Zoom hung up the telephone, stalked out of the back door of the house and into the garage where his coupé and his police dog awaited him.

The dog thumped his tail in greeting.

Zoom jumped into the car, opened the garage doors, started the motor and purred out into the night.

IIc drove directly to the lot where the rubbish had been dumped, a marshy hollow, surrounded with scattered dwellings of a cheaper sort, fringed with clumps of brush.

Sidney Zoom opened the back of the coupé and took out a straw figure. He sat this figure against the steering wheel, clamped his hat upon it, turned on the dome light, and walked briskly down the sidewalk and into the shadows of a clump of brush. The police dog padded at his side.

The silence of the night enveloped them.

Far away, there was a sleepy rumble from the slumbering city where heavy trucks or belated passenger cars ground their way through the main boulevards. Once there was the whine of a motor coming at high speed, but that sound abruptly died away.

Minutes passed.

Sidney Zoom yawned. The dog flexed his muscles, wagged his tail.

There was the distant wail of a siren.

Some sound, inaudible to the ears of the man, caused the dog to stiffen to rigid attention. His ears pricked forward. He crouched, muscles as tense as steel wires.

"Steady, Rip," warned Sidney Zoom in a whisper.

A low, warning growl came from the dog, ceased when Zoom's hand pressed down upon his head.

Motionless, tense, the two waited, master and dog.

Bang!

The darkness spurted flame. There was the crash of glass.

It was a rifle shot, and the stabbing flash had come from some fifty yards across the pile of rubbish, from a dense clump of brush.

Bang!

A second shot, fired with slow deliberation.

Glass tinkled and a window of the coupé collapsed. A great square of glass fell to the sidewalk.

Bang!

The third shot thudded into the straw figure, sent it hurtling to the seat of the coupé.

Sidney Zoom took his hand from the neck of the police dog.

"All right, Rip," he said.

The dog went into the darkness like a streak of shadow, stomach close to the ground.

Bang! sounded the rifle.

A siren wailed.

Zoom was running now, his hawklike eyes penetrating the darkness sufficiently to show him the obstacles to be avoided. But the dog was far ahead, running with padded feet that made no noise, guided by eyes that were as accustomed to the darkness as the eyes of a wolf.

Zoom heard a throaty growl from the night.

A man screamed.

There was the thudding impact of flesh against flesh and the sound of a body striking the ground.

The siren wailed close at hand. A police car, red spotlight glowing like a red pool of fire, swung around the corner.

Bang! went the rifle for the last shot, such a shot as might have been the result of a cocked rifle having been dashed to the ground.

Zoom ran toward that shot, his long legs covering the ground rapidly.

"Steady, Rip," he warned.

The police car applied brakes and wheels screamed along the pavement. The spotlight shifted its ruddy beam to the lot, showing a huddled figure on the ground, the form of the police dog crouched a little bit to one side.

Sidney Zoom shouted and burst into the circle of illumination, waving his hands.

The door of the police car banged open as two figures sprinted for the place where the still figure lay on the ground. Zoom was the first to arrive.

A second later Lieutenant Sylvester, accompanied by Captain Mahoney, produced a pocket flashlight and sent the brilliant white beam down on that which lay upon the ground.

"Wetler!" exclaimed Mahoney.

"Wetler," said Zoom.

Mahoney knelt by the man.

"You murdered Stanwood?" asked Captain Mahoney. "You're dying. Better tell the truth."

Wetler nodded, groaned.

"Why?" asked Mahoney.

"Wanted money . . . under will . . . damned miser!
. . . Dog knocked me over . . . rifle went off . . ."

"Why did you use a wax figure?"

"Afraid police . . . might trace car took him away in . . .
wanted make sure to blame it on the girl . . . hated her . . .
snooty . . . stuck up . . ."

The figure twitched and lay still.

Captain Mahoney got to his feet.

"That seems to be the end of it," he said. "I suppose your
call to Sylvester was intended to be overheard by Wetler?"

Zoom nodded.

"I used the wax for a third degree. I knew the murderer
would become alarmed when he saw there was wax on his
shoes or slippers. He would never think I had trapped him to
walk on the wax, but would think I had doped out the solution of the crime and suspected him.

"Naturally, he would listen to my telephone conversation,
then follow me, hoping to get a chance to kill me before I
could tell what I knew. So I left a dummy for him to shoot at
and relied on the dog to drag him down. I hadn't figured on
the man being killed. But it's a good thing. Saved the execu-
tioner a job. Frankly, I'm glad of it."

Captain Mahoney sighed and stared at Zoom curiously.

"A reasoning machine," he commented, "devoid of sympathy."

"Sympathy, bah! That's the trouble with the world's atti-
tude toward the criminal. Sympathy! Here is a man who
planned murder, planned to pin it on an innocent young
woman, and you prate of sympathy!"

"You're not strong for mercy, for a fact," commented
Lieutenant Sylvester.

Sidney Zoom raised his strong, rugged features.

"No," he said in a tone that was almost dreamy, "I simply

see mercy from a broader standpoint. For instance, from the standpoint of an innocent young woman accused of crime. And, perhaps, I see a little more in this than you do."

"Such as?" asked Lieutenant Sylvester.

"Such as divine justice, for instance," said Sidney Zoom, and turned on his heel.

"Come, Rip," he called to the dog. "Our work here is finished."

And, followed by the padding feet of the tawny police dog, he stalked away into the chill shadows of the night, walking with that catfooted sureness of motion.

The Affair of the Reluctant Witness

JERRY BANE knuckled his eyes into wakefulness, kicked back the covers and said, "What time is it, Mugs?"

"Ten-thirty," Mugs Magoo told him.

Bane jumped from the bed, stood in front of the open window and went through a series of quick calisthenics.

Magoo surveyed the swift, lithe motions with eyes that had been trained to soak in details as a fresh blotting paper absorbs ink.

Jerry Bane straightened, extended his arms from the shoulder and, bending his knees, rapidly raised and lowered his body.

"How am I doing, Mugs?"

"Okay," Magoo said without enthusiasm. "I guess you just ain't the type that puts on weight. What's your waist?"

"Twenty-eight."

Mugs's comment was based on fifty years of cynical observation. "It's all right while you're young," he said, "and the girls are crazy about a good dancer, to be slim-waisted, but when you get up to what I call the competitive years, it takes beef to flatten out the opposition. When I was on the police force, the boys used to figure you needed weight to have impact. Not fat, you understand, but beef and bone."

161

"I understand," Bane said, smiling.

Mugs surveyed the empty sleeve of his right arm. "Of course," he added, "I've only got one punch now, but that one punch will do the work if I can get it in the right place and at the right time. What do you want for breakfast?"

"Poached eggs and coffee. What's the right time for the punch, Mugs?"

"First," Mugs said laconically.

Jerry chuckled.

"Better take your orange juice before you have your shower," Mugs advised, "and remember your friend, Arthur Arman Anson, is coming this morning."

Bane laughed. "Don't call that old fossil a friend. He's an attorney and the executor of my uncle's estate, that's all. He disapproves thoroughly of everything I do. . . . What's in the mail?"

"Did you order a package of photos from the Shooting Star News Photo Service?"

Bane nodded.

Mugs cocked a quizzical eyebrow.

"It's an idea I had," Jerry said. "It's the answer to Anson, Mugs. The Shooting Star outfit has photographers who cover all the news events. Now, with your photographic memory, your knowledge of the underworld, the confidence men, the slickers and the hypocrites, it occurred to me it might be a good plan for us to study the news photographs. In other words, Mugs, we might build up a business, an unorthodox business, to be sure, but a profitable business."

"And a dangerous business?" Mugs asked.

Jerry merely grinned that one off.

"It's an expensive service?" Mugs asked dryly.

"A hundred bucks a month," Jerry said cheerfully. "Do you know, Mugs, Arthur Arman Anson had the colossal effrontery to tell me that since he's the trustee of a so-called spendthrift trust under my uncle's will he can withhold every penny of the trust fund if he sees fit.

"The ten thousand we got in a lump sum from my uncle's estate must be about gone. Anson is going to be difficult, so I thought we'd better do a little sharpshooting. He lives by his brains. We'll live by our wits."

"I see," Mugs said without expression.

"That ten grand *is* about gone, isn't it?" Jerry asked.

Mugs headed for the kitchenette. "I think I'd better look at the coffee."

"Okay," Bane said cheerfully.

He seated himself in front of the mirror, opened the package of photographs Mugs brought him, drank his orange juice, then connected the electric shaver.

Magoo said, "Anson is going to be here any minute now. Hope you don't mind my saying so, but he won't like it if he finds you still in pajamas. It irritates him."

"I know," Jerry said. "The old fossil thinks he has a right to order my life just because he's the executor of a spendthrift trust. How much money is left in the account, Mugs?"

Magoo cleared his throat. "I can't remember exactly," he said.

Bane disconnected the razor so that he could hear better. "Mugs, what the devil's the matter?"

"Nothing."

"*Phooey!* Let's have it."

"I'm sorry," Magoo blurted, "but you're overdrawn three hundred and eighty-seven dollars. The bank sent a notice."

"I suppose the bank also advised Arthur Anson," Jerry said, "and he's coming up to pour reproaches over me and rub them in the open wounds."

"He'll relent and tide you over," Mugs said without conviction. "That's why your uncle made him trustee."

"Not Anson. That old petrified pretzel wants to run my

life. If I'd do what he wants I'd become another Arthur
Arman Anson, puttering around with a briefcase, a cavern-
ous, bony face, lips as thin as a safety-razor blade, and about
as sharp. . . . Well, Mugs, I don't know what I'm going to do
about salary, and today, I believe, is payday."

"You don't need to bother about salary," Magoo said feel-
ingly. "When you picked me up I was selling pencils on the
street."

"It isn't a question of what you *were* doing, but what you
are doing," Jerry said. "Well, we'll finish with the whiskers,
then the shower, then breakfast, then finances."

He resumed his shaving and as he did so started studying
the pictures which had been sent out by the Shooting Star
News Photo Service, photographs on eight-by-ten, with a
hard, glossy finish, each photograph bearing a mimeo-
graphed warning to watch the credit line and a brief description of the picture so that news editors could make and run
their own captions.

Jerry Bane tossed aside a picture of an automobile accident. "I guess the idea of this picture stuff wasn't so good,
Mugs. It seems they're running around like mad, shooting
auto accidents with all of the gruesome details."

"Part of a publicity campaign to educate the people,"
Mugs explained.

"Well, *those* photographs certainly don't interest me,"
Bane said. "Here, Mugs, you're the camera-eye man of the
outfit. Run your eye through these pictures while I shower. I
can't look at gruesome, mangled bodies and smashed-up automobiles on an empty stomach. See if you can't find the picture of some crook who's crashed into the news, someone you
can tell me about. Then we may be able to figure out an
angle."

Mugs said deprecatingly, "Of course, I'm an old-timer, Mr.

Bane. There's a whole crop of newcomers in the crime field since I—"

"I know," Bane interrupted, laughing. "You're always apologizing, but the fact remains you have the old camera eye. That's where you got your nickname, Mugs, from being able to remember faces. They tell me you've never forgotten a face, a name, or a connection."

"That was in the old days, sir. I had both arms then and I was on the force and—"

"Yes, yes, I know," Jerry interrupted hastily, "and then you got mixed up in politics. Then you lost an arm, took to drink, and wound up selling pencils."

"There was an interval with a gentleman by the name of Mr. Pry," Mugs Magoo said somewhat wistfully. "He was a fast worker, that lad—reminds me of you. But I got to drinking too much and—"

"Well, you're on the wagon now," Bane said reassuringly, studying the reflection of his face in the mirror. "Guess that's got the whiskers off okay. I'll take a shower, then eat breakfast. You look over these pictures and see if you find anyone you know."

Still clad in pajamas, Bane seated himself at the breakfast table and said, "What about the photographs, Mugs?"

Magoo said, "A neat bit of cheesecake, sir. You might prefer this to the auto-accident pictures."

"Let's take a look."

Mugs Magoo passed over the picture of a girl in a bathing suit.

Bane looked at the picture, then read the caption underneath aloud:

"Federal Court proceedings were enlivened yesterday when, during a bathing-suit patent case, Stella Darling, nightclub entertainer, modeled the suit. 'Remove the garment and it will be introduced as plaintiff's Exhibit A,' said Judge Asa Lansing, then added hastily, 'Not here! Not here!' while the courtroom rocked with laughter."

Bane surveyed the photograph. "Some babe!"

Mugs nodded.

"Nice chassis."

Again Mugs nodded.

"But somehow the face doesn't go with the legs," Bane said. "It's a sad face, almost tragic. That expression could have been carved on a wooden mask."

Mugs Magoo said, "Nice kid when I first knew her. Won a beauty contest and was Miss Something-or-other in nineteen forty-three. Then things happened to her fast. She cashed in on what prosperity she could get, married a pretty good chap, then fell in love with another guy. Her husband caught her cheating, shot the other man, couldn't get by with the unwritten law and went to jail. She came out West and turned up in the nightclubs. Nice figure, but gossip followed her from back East. Too bad the kid can't get a break and begin all over again. Gossip has long legs."

Bane nodded thoughtfully. "When you come right down to it, Mugs, there's not so much to differentiate her from a lot of the people who look down on her."

"Just a mere thirty minutes," Magoo said. "How's your coffee?"

"The coffee's fine. Why the thirty minutes, Mugs?"

"Her husband's train could have been late, sir."

Bane grinned. "What else, Mugs? Anything else?"

"One here I don't get," Mugs said.

"What is it?"

Mugs handed him a photograph. It showed a young woman standing in a serve-yourself grocery store, pointing an accusing finger at a broad-shouldered man who, in turn, was pointing an accusing finger at the woman. At the woman's feet a dog lay sprawled. A pile of groceries on the counter by the cash register were evidently purchases made by the man.

"Why the double pointing?" Bane asked.

"Read it," Mugs said.

Bane read the caption:

ACCUSER ACCUSED—In a strange double mix-up yesterday afternoon, Bernice Calhoun, 23, 9305 Sunset Way, accused William L. Gordon, 32, residing at a rooming house at 505 Monadnock Drive, of having held up a jewelry shop known as the Jewel Casket, 9316 Sunset Way. When the suspect entered her Serve-Yourself Grocery Store, Miss Calhoun notified police, explaining she had seen Gordon, carrying a gun, backing out of the jewelry shop, forcing the proprietor, Harvey Haggard, to hold his hands high in the air. Then Gordon, alarmed by an approaching prowl car, entered the grocery store, apparently as a customer, picked up a shopping basket and started selecting canned goods. Police, answering Bernice Calhoun's call, rushed to the scene, only to encounter complications. Not only was no loot found on Gordon, but Harvey Haggard, casually reading a magazine in the Jewel Casket, said it was all news to him. So far as he knew, no one had staged a stick-up. Gordon accused the woman of blackmail and is starting suit for defamation of character. Bernice Calhoun, who is well liked in the neighborhood and who inherited the grocery store from her father, is frankly disturbed over her predicament. This photograph was taken just a few minutes after police arrived on the scene and shows Bernice Calhoun, right, accusing Gordon, left, who is, in turn, accusing Miss Calhoun. Gordon was taken into custody by police, pending an investigation.

"Now that," Bane said, "is *something!* Know anything about it, Mugs?"

"This Gordon," Mugs said, placing a stubby finger on the picture of the man, "is a slick one. They call him 'Gopher'

Gordon because he's always burrowing and working in the dark."

"You think it's a frame-up to shake Bernice Calhoun loose from some change?"

"More probably Gopher Gordon and Harvey Haggard are standing in together and want to get the grocery-store lease."

"Seems a rather crude way of doing it," Bane said.

"Anything that works ain't crude," Mugs insisted doggedly.

"I wish you'd look into this, Mugs," Jerry Bane said thoughtfully. "It has possibilities. Here we are fresh out of cash, and this crook . . . and a beautiful woman . . . Check up on it, will you, Mugs?"

"You want me to do it now?"

"Right now," Jerry Bane said. "The way I look at it, haste is important. Get started."

Ten minutes after Mugs Magoo had left, Arthur Arman Anson knocked on the door.

His cold knuckles tapped with evenly spaced decision.

Jerry Bane let him in.

"Hello, Counselor," he said. "I've just finished breakfast. How about having a cup of coffee?"

"No, thank you. I breakfasted at six-thirty."

"You look it," Bane said.

"How's that?"

"I said you looked it. You know, early to bed, early to rise, and all that sort of stuff."

Anson settled himself with severe austerity in a straight-backed chair, depositing his briefcase beside him.

"I come in the performance of a necessary but disagreeable duty," Anson said, his voice showing that he relished his errand, despite his remarks.

"Go right ahead with the lecture," Jerry Bane said.

"It's not a lecture, young man. I am merely making a few remarks."

"Go ahead and make them, then, but remember the adjective."

"You are living the life of a wastrel. By this time you should have recovered from the harrowing experiences of the Japanese prison camp. You should have recovered from the effects of your two years of malnutrition. In other words, young man, you should go to work."

"What do you suggest?" Jerry asked.

"Hard, manual labor," Anson said grimly.

"I don't get it."

"That is the way *I* got *my* start. I worked with pick and shovel on railroad construction and—"

"And then inherited money, I believe," Jerry said.

"That has nothing to do with it, young man. I began at the bottom and have worked my way to the top. You are wasting your time in frivolity. I don't suppose you go to bed before eleven or twelve o'clock at night! I find you at this hour of the morning still lounging around in pajamas.

"Furthermore, I find you associating with a disreputable character, a one-armed consort of the underworld, who has sold pencils on the streets of this city."

"He's loyal and I like him," Jerry said.

"He's a dissipated has-been," Anson snapped. "Your uncle left you ten thousand dollars outright. The bulk of his estate, however, he left to me as trustee. I am empowered to give you as much or as little of that money as I see fit, the idea being that—"

"Yes, yes, I know," Jerry interrupted. "My uncle thought I might spend it all in one wild fling. He wanted you to see that it was passed out to me in installments. All right, I'm broke right now. Pass out an installment."

"I do not know what your uncle wanted," Anson said, "but I do know what I intend to do."

"What's that?"

"You have squandered the ten thousand dollars. Look at this apartment, equipped with vacuum cleaners, electric dishwashers, all sorts of gadgets. . . ."

"Because my man has only one arm, and I'm trying to—"

"Exactly. Because of your sentiment for this sodden hulk of the streets, you have dissipated your cash inheritance. Young man, the bank advises me you are overdrawn. Now then, I'm going to give it to you straight. Get out of this apartment. Go to a rooming house somewhere, and start living within your means. Strip off those tailored clothes, get into overalls, start doing hard, manual labor. At the end of six months I will again discuss the matter with you. . . . Do you know how much you have spent in the last three months?"

"I never was much good at addition," Jerry confessed.

"Try subtraction then!" Anson snapped.

Bane's face was reproachful. "Just when I was about to steer a lawsuit to your office—a spectacular case you're bound to win."

Anson's shrewd eyes showed a brief flicker of interest. "What's the case?"

"I can't tell you now."

"Bosh. Probably something I wouldn't touch with a ten-foot pole. And in any event, my decision would remain unaltered."

"A beautiful case," Bane went on. "A case involving defamation of character. The young woman defendant is entirely innocent. You'll have an opportunity to walk into court and make one of those spectacular, last-minute exposés of the other side. A case that has everything."

"Who is this client?"

"A raving, roaring beauty."

"I don't want them to rave. I don't want them to roar. I want them to pay," Anson said, and then added, "And I don't care whether they're beautiful, or not."

Bane grinned. "But think of it, Anson. All this, and beauty too."

"Don't think you can bribe me, young man. I have been an attorney too long to fall for these blandishments, these nebulous fees which never materialize, these mysterious clients with their marvelous cases who somehow never quite get to the office. You have my ultimatum. I'll thank you to advise me within forty-eight hours that you have gone to work. Hard manual labor. At the end of what I consider a proper period I will then give you a chance to get a so-called white-collar job. Good day, sir."

"And you won't have a cup of coffee?"

"Definitely not. I never eat between meals."

Arthur Arman Anson slammed the door behind him.

Mugs Magoo found Jerry Bane sprawled out in the big easy chair, his mind completely absorbed in a book entitled *The Mathematics of Business Management.* Beside him on the smoking stand was a slide rule with which Bane had been checking the conclusions of the author.

Magoo stood by the chair for some two or three minutes before Bane, feeling his presence, fidgeted uneasily for a moment, then looked up.

"I didn't want to interrupt you," Mugs said, "but I have a very interesting story."

"You talked with her?"

"Yes."

"Is she really as good-looking as the newspaper picture made her out to be?"

Mugs took a photograph from an envelope. "Better. This was taken last summer at a beach resort."

Jerry Bane carefully studied the picture, then gave a low whistle.

"Exactly," Mugs Magoo said dryly.

"Now how the devil did you get this, Mugs?"

Magoo said, "Well, I found that the store's about all she has in the world and she's pretty hard up for cash. I told her some of the big wholesalers were going to put on a campaign to feature neighborhood grocery stores and they wanted to get pictures that would catch the eye. I told her that if she had an attractive picture of herself, one that would look well in print, she might win a prize, and that if she did, a man would come to photograph the store and pay her a hundred and fifty dollars for the right to publish her picture; that if the picture wasn't used, she'd get it back and wouldn't be out anything."

Jerry Bane studied the picture. "Plenty of this and that and these and those. Lots of oomph, Mugs."

"Plenty, sir."

"And she's hard up for cash?"

"Apparently so. She wants to sell the store, but she's worried about what may happen on this defamation of character suit."

"What's new in that case, Mugs?"

"Well, she's beginning to think she may have acted a little hastily. She isn't *certain* she saw the gun. She saw the man throw something over the fence, but the police haven't been able to find anything. Frankly, sir, I think she's beginning to feel she was mistaken. . . . But she wasn't."

"She wasn't?"

Mugs Magoo shook his head. "I got a look at this man, Haggard, who runs that jewelry store. I know some stuff about him the police don't."

"What?"

"He's a fence, and he's clever as hell. He buys stuff here and ships it by air express to retail outlets all over the country."

"An association of fences?"

Mugs nodded and said, "You can figure out what happened. This man Gordon had probably had some dealings with Haggard and had been given a doublecross. He decided to get even in his own way."

Bane nodded thoughtfully. "So, naturally, Haggard can't admit anything was taken because he doesn't dare describe the loot. . . . Let me take a look at that picture again, Mugs."

Mugs handed him the photograph of the girl in the bathing suit.

"Not that one," Jerry Bane said. "The one that shows her accusing Gopher Gordon, and Gopher Gordon accusing her. Do you know, Mugs, I'm beginning to get a very definite idea that may pay off."

"I thought you might," Magoo said. "A man can look at a picture of a jane like that and get ideas pretty fast."

The girl looked up from the cash register as Jerry entered the store.

Jerry noticed that she had a nice complexion and good lines, because he was something of an expert in such matters. Her long, slender legs had just the right curves in keeping with her streamlined figure. Moreover, there was a certain alertness in her eyes, a mischievous, provocative something which held a definite challenge.

Jerry Bane, apparently completely preoccupied with his errand, picked up a market basket and walked around looking at the canned goods.

"Could I help you?" Bernice Calhoun asked somewhat archly, her eyes making approving appraisal.

"No, thank you."

Bane moved on in his preoccupied manner, carefully studying the various kinds of canned goods.

The girl tossed her head and returned to an inspection of the accounts on which she had been working when Jerry entered. This slack time of the afternoon was a period which she apparently set aside for her bookkeeping.

Left to his own devices, Jerry carefully selected a can of grapefruit and a package of rolled oats. He glanced back toward the cans of dog food on the counter where the girl bent over her work beside the cash register—the cans which had shown up so plainly in the news photo. Then he looked at his watch. Very soon—almost at once, in fact, if Mugs Magoo was on the beam—the telephone would ring and Bernice Calhoun would leave the counter to answer it. If Mugs could keep her there for a minute or two, there would be time enough for . . .

The phone shrilled. The girl looked up. Her eyes rested briefly on Jerry, then she slammed the cash-register drawer shut with a clang and walked swiftly to the back of the store, where the telephone hung on the wall in a corner.

Jerry stepped in front of the pyramided cans of dog food. They were arranged so that the labels were toward the front —except for one can. He deftly extracted this can from the pile.

The lid had been entirely removed by the use of a can opener which had made a smooth job of cutting around the top of the can. The interior contained bits of dried dog food still adhering to the tin, but, in addition to that, there was a flash of scintillating brilliance, light shafts from sparkling gems which showed ruby red, emerald green and the indescribable glitter of diamonds.

Jerry's body shielded what he was doing from the girl. His hand, moving swiftly, dumped the contents of the can into an inside coat pocket, a coruscating cascade of unset jewels which rattled reassuringly.

From another pocket in his coat, he took some cheap imitation jewels which he had removed from costume jewelry. When he had the can two-thirds full, he took some of the genuine stones and placed them on top in a layer of brilliant temptation.

He replaced the can, being careful to leave it just as he had found it, then wandered over to the shelf where the jams were displayed. As he picked up a jar of marmalade, he heard the girl's footsteps clicking back to the counter. He took his basket of groceries to her.

She seemed now to have definitely decided upon an impersonal course of conduct.

"Good afternoon," she said politely, and viciously jabbed at the keys of the cash register. "Two dollars and sixteen cents," she announced.

Jerry gravely handed her a five-dollar bill. She rang up the sale on the cash register.

"Too bad about your lawsuit," Jerry said. "I have an idea I can help you."

She was engaged in making change, but stopped and glanced up at him swiftly. "What's *your* game?" she asked.

"No game. I only thought I might be of some assistance."

"In what way?"

"I have a friend who is a very able lawyer."

"Oh, *that!*" She shrugged contemptuously.

"And, if I spoke to him, I'm quite sure he'd handle your case for a nominal fee."

She laughed scornfully. "I know, just because I have an honest face—or is it the figure?"

Jerry Bane said, "Perhaps I'd better explain myself. I have reason to believe you're being victimized."

"Indeed," she said, her voice as cutting as a cold wind on a wintry evening. "Your perspicacity surprises me, Mr.—er—"

"Mr. Bane," he said. "Jerry to my friends."

"Oh, yes, *Mister* Bane!"

"While you probably don't realize it," Jerry went on, "the man whom you identified as the stickup artist is known to the police of the northern cities. He doesn't have a criminal record in the sense that his fingerprints have ever been taken, and no one knows him here, but the police in the north know a little about him."

"Wouldn't that be valuable in—well, you know, in the event he sues me for defamation of character?" she asked, her voice suddenly friendly.

"It would be more than valuable. It would be priceless."

"You have proof?"

"I think I can get proof."

She slowly closed the drawer of the cash register. "Exactly what is it you want?" she asked.

Jerry made a little gesture of dismissal. "Merely an opportunity to be of service."

"Phooey!"

"Try me out."

"If I do, I'll hold you to your promise."

"I'd expect you to."

"What do you want me to do?"

"First, tell me exactly what happened—everything."

She studied him thoughtfully, then said abruptly, "Ever since my father died, I've been trying to make a go of this place. It won't warrant paying the salary of a clerk. It's a small place. I have to do the work myself.

"I keep track of the stock. I make up orders. I keep books.

I open shipments, arrange the stock on the shelves and do all
sorts of odd jobs. I work here at night and early in the morning. During the daytime I fill in the time between customers
with clerical work on the books.

"Day before yesterday I happened to be looking out of
that window. From this position you can look right across to
that little jewelry shop known as the Jewel Casket.

"I don't know much about that place. Now that I think of
it, I don't know how a person could expect to make a living
with a jewelry store in that location, but Mr. Haggard evidently does all right. Of course, he doesn't have a high rent
to pay.

"Well, anyway, as I was looking out of the window, I saw
this man's back and I felt certain he was holding a gun. I
thought I could see someone in the store holding his hands
up. Then this man, Gordon, came out into the street, and
I'm almost positive he tossed something over the board fence
into that vacant lot.

"Then I saw him stiffen with apprehension and he seemed
to be ready to run. I couldn't see what had frightened him at
the moment, but I could see he was looking over his left
shoulder, up the street."

"Go on," Jerry said.

"Well, he didn't run. He hurried across the street over
here. Just as he came in the door, I saw what it was that had
frightened him."

"What was it?"

"A police prowl car. It came cruising by, going slowly, the
red spotlight on the windshield and the radio antennae showing plainly it was a police car. I was frightened, simply scared
stiff."

"You have a dog here?" Bane asked.

"Yes, but he's a good-natured, friendly dog. He would be

no protection unless, perhaps, someone should manhandle me."

"What did this man do after he got inside here?"

"Walked around the store and tried to act like a customer, picking out canned goods to put in a basket, but picking them out carefully and with such attention to the labels that I knew he was simply stalling.

"I guess I was in such a panic that I didn't stop to think—I just don't know. At the time I really felt he was a stick-up man. Now I'm not so sure. Anyhow, I went to the phone and got police headquarters. The phone's so far back in the store," she explained, "that he couldn't hear me from where he was."

Jerry nodded. "Not very convenient to have it so far away. Usually, I mean—for orders and that sort of thing."

"I don't take phone orders," she said. "That's what I kept trying to tell that guy that called just now. But he couldn't seem to understand. Maybe because he was English. You know, very lah-de-dah kind of voice."

Jerry grinned. Mugs and his imitation of Jeeves! He'd do it at the drop of a hat.

"So you called the police," he prompted the girl.

"Yes. I told them who I was, explained that a man had just held up the jewelry store across the street, had been frightened by a police radio car and had taken refuge in my store. I knew that the police department could get in touch with the radio car right away and I suggested they have the driver turn around and come back here."

"And that was done?"

"Yes. It took them about—oh, I'd say four or five minutes."

"And what happened when the police arrived?"

"The car pulled up in front of the store. The officers

jumped out with drawn guns, and I pointed out this man to them and accused him of having held up the store across the street.

"At that time the man had finished buying his groceries and was standing here at the cash register. I'd been fumbling around a bit making his change, so that the radio car would have time to get back.

"This man said his name was Gordon and that I was crazy, that he'd stopped to look in the window of the Jewel Casket, had started to go in to buy a present for his girl friend, and then changed his mind and decided to buy some groceries instead. He said that he'd never carried a gun in his life. The police searched him and found nothing. I told them to go over to the Jewel Casket. I thought perhaps they'd find Mr. Haggard dead."

"What happened?"

She said, "That's the part I simply can't understand. Mr. Haggard was there in the store and he said that no one had been in during the last fifteen minutes and that he hadn't been held up. I—I felt like a complete ninny."

"Would you gamble a little of your time and do *exactly* what I say if it would get you out of this mess?" Bane asked.

"What do you want?"

"I want you to close up the store and come with me to see my lawyer, Arthur Anson. I want you to tell him your story. After that I want you to promise me that, in case he should return to the store with you, you'll stay right beside him all the time he's here."

"Why that?" she asked.

Jerry grinned. "It's just a hunch. Do *just* as I tell you and you may get this cleaned up."

She thought that over for several seconds, then said, "Oh, well, what have I got to lose?"

"Exactly," Jerry said, and his smile was like spring sunshine.

Arthur Arman Anson was cold as a wet towel.

"Jerry, I'm a busy man. I have no time to listen to your wheedling. I will not give you—"

"I told your secretary that I have a client waiting," Jerry Bane interrupted.

"I recognize the typical approach," Anson said. "I not only fear the Greeks when they bear gifts, but I shall not change my decision in your case by so much as a single, solitary penny! Kindly remember that."

Jerry Bane whipped the bathing suit photograph out of his briefcase. "This is a picture of the client."

Arthur Anson adjusted his glasses and peered through the lower segments of his bifocals at the photograph. He *harrumphed* importantly.

Jerry Bane whipped out the other photograph, the one taken by the Shooting Star photographer, and said, "Take a look at *that* picture. Study the caption."

Arthur Anson looked at the photograph, read the caption, and once more cleared his throat.

"Interesting," he said noncommittally, and then added after a moment, "Very."

"Now then," Jerry Bane went on, "this man, Mugs Magoo, who works for me—"

"A thoroughly disreputable character," Anson interrupted.

"—has a camera eye and a great memory," Bane went on as though the interruption had not been made. "As soon as he looked at this picture he recognized this man as a crook."

"Indeed!"

"He's known as Gopher Gordon because he works underground and by such devious methods the police have never been able to get anything on him. This is the first time he's actually been held for anything and the first time he's ever been fingerprinted. That's why he's so furious at Bernice, and so determined to sue her."

Anson stroked the long angle of his jaw with the tips of bony fingers. "A bad reputation is a very difficult thing to prove. People don't want to get on the witness stand and testify. However, of course, if this young woman insists upon consulting me, and if she has sufficient funds to pay me an ample retainer as well as to hire competent detectives—"

"She isn't going to pay you a cent," Jerry Bane said.

Sheer surprise jerked Arthur Anson out of his professional calm. "What's that?"

"She isn't going to pay you a cent."

Anson pushed back the photographs. "Then get her out of my office," he stormed. "Damn it, Bane, I—"

"But," Jerry interrupted, "you're going to make a lot of money out of the case just the same, because you're going to get such a spectacular courtroom victory it'll give you an enormous amount of advertising."

"I don't need advertising."

"A man can't get too much of it," Jerry said, talking rapidly. "Now, look what happened. This man Haggard says he *wasn't* held up. Bernice knows that he was. He's lying. You can tear into him on cross-examination and—"

"And prove my client is a liar."

"I tell you she isn't a liar. She's a sweet young girl who is being victimized."

Anson shook his head decisively. "If this jewelry store man says he wasn't held up, that finishes it. This young woman is a blackmailer and a liar. Get her out of my office."

Jerry Bane said desperately, "I wish you'd listen to me. These men are both crooks."

"*Both?*"

"Yes, both. They have to be."

"Indeed," Anson said with elaborate irony. "Simply because these men tell a story which fails to coincide with that told by a young woman with whom you have apparently become infatuated—"

"Don't you see?" Jerry interrupted once more. "Haggard is running a jewelry store out there in a neighborhood where the volume would be too small to support his overhead unless the store were a mask for some illegitimate activity. Out there he poses as a small operator, selling cheap jewelry to a family trade, costume jewelry to schoolgirls, fountain pens, cigarette lighters, various knick-knacks. Actually he has a more sinister and more profitable activity. He's a fence.

"Being out in that district of small neighborhood stores, he's in a position to keep irregular hours. No one thinks anything of it when he comes down at night and putters around in his store, because many of the storekeepers who can't afford much help do the same thing. So Haggard uses this fact as a shield for an illicit business.

"This man Gordon is a crook. Gordon knew what Haggard's business was. He undoubtedly knew that some very large haul of stones had been purchased by Haggard, and Gordon saw a chance to step in and clean up. He knew that Haggard wouldn't be in a position to report his loss to the police. Gordon was personally unknown to Haggard, just as he is unknown to the police here. He hoped that no one who had known him in the north would catch up with him and identify him.

"An ordinary crook, established here in this city, wouldn't have dared to hold up a fence. The underworld has its own way of meting out punishment. But Gordon was an outsider, a slick worker, a man who could step in, make a stickup, and then get out. He's noted for that. He's called the 'Gopher.' "

"And what did he do with the loot?" Anson asked sarcastically. "Remember, the police searched him."

"Sure, the police searched him. But he'd been in that grocery store for some five minutes before they searched him, and he saw the young woman go over to the telephone and start talking in a low tone of voice. He wasn't so dumb but what he knew that he was trapped. His only chance was to get rid of the jewelry."

"Where did he put it?"

"It's concealed in various places around the store. . . . Why, look here!" Jerry said in sudden excitement, as though the idea had just occurred to him. "What would have prevented him from buying a can opener, opening a can, dumping out the contents and putting the jewelry in the empty can?"

"Ah, yes," Anson said, his voice a cold sneer. "The typical reasoning of a fat-brained, young spendthrift. I suppose he opened a can of peaches, dumped the peaches on the floor, and then put the jewelry in the can. The police searched the place and couldn't find anything wrong. They never noticed the dripping can or the peaches on the floor. Oh, no!"

"Well," Bane said desperately, "it wouldn't need to have been a can of peaches. And he could have opened a can so neatly that . . . Why, suppose he'd opened a can of dog food and put that on the floor! The dog would promptly have gulped it up and . . . Say, wait a minute—"

Jerry broke off to look at the photograph with eyes that were suddenly wide with surprise, as though he were just noticing something he hadn't seen before. "Look right here!" he said. "There's canned dog food, piled on the counter. And —yes—here's one can that's turned around, turned the wrong way so the brand name doesn't show."

Anson was now studying the photograph too. Jerry pointed to the pile of groceries on the counter. "And look at what he has there! A can opener! That settles it. He picked up the can opener—I saw them on a box by the canned fruit shelves when I was there; they're a quarter apiece—and he used it on the can of dog food. Probably while the girl was at the back of the store phoning the police. It—"

Anson snatched the photographs out of Jerry Bane's hand and popped them into a drawer in his desk. "Young man," he said, "your reasoning is asinine, puerile, sophomoric, and absurd. However, you have brought a young woman to my office, a young woman who is in a legal predicament. I will, at least, talk with her. I will not judge her entirely on the strength of what you may say."

"Very well, I'll call her in," Jerry said, his voice without expression.

"You'll do nothing of the sort, young man. I do not discuss business with clients in the presence of an outsider. You have brought this woman to my office. I will talk with her and I will talk with her privately. I'll excuse you now, Mr. Bane— and naturally I'll expect you to keep this entire matter entirely confidential."

"Any need for secrecy?"

"It's *not* secrecy. It's merely preserving the legal integrity of my office. Good afternoon, young man."

"Good afternoon, sir," Jerry said.

Jerry Bane found Stella Darling waiting impatiently.

"Your phone call said you had a modeling job," she said. "I've been waiting here for over an hour."

"Sorry, I was a little late," Jerry said. "I was making arrangements with my clients."

"What sort of a modeling job is it?"

"Well," Jerry said, "to be frank with you, Miss Darling, it's just a bit out of the ordinary. It's—"

Her voice cut across his like a knife. "Nude?" she asked.

"No, no. Nothing like that."

"How did you find out about me?" she asked.

"I saw the photograph of you modeling the bathing suit in court."

"I see." Her voice indicated that she saw a great deal. Her appraisal of Jerry Bane was personal and, after a moment, approving.

Jerry said, "This job is one I'd like to have you carry out to the letter. I have here a sheet of typewritten instructions, telling you just what to do."

She said, "Look, Mr. Bane, I have a lot of things put up to me. I'm trying to make a living. I have a beautiful body. I'm trying to capitalize on it while it lasts. I made the mistake of winning a beauty contest once and thought I was going to become a movie star overnight. I quit school and started signing up with this and that. . . . Lord, what I wouldn't give to turn back the hands of the clock and be back in school once more!"

"Perhaps," Jerry said, "if you do *exactly* as I say, you'll have an opportunity to do that. I'm trying a unique exploitation of a brand-new dog food. If things go the way I want, I may be able to sell out the brand and the good will, lock, stock and barrel.

"However, I haven't time to discuss details now. Here's some money to cover your regular hourly rate. If you do a good job, you'll receive a substantial bonus tomorrow. Now then, get busy."

"And I wear street clothes?"

"Street clothes," Jerry Bane said. "Just what you have on."

She sized him up, then said, "The modeling I have been doing has been—well, it's been a little bit of everything. You don't need to be afraid to tell me what it is. You don't need to write it out for me. Just go ahead and tell me."

Jerry Bane smiled and shook his head. "Read these typewritten instructions," he said. "Follow them to the letter and get started."

She took the typewritten sheet from him, once more gave him a glance from under long-lashed eyelids. "Okay," she said, "I'll do it your way."

Jerry Bane hailed a taxicab. "You'll have to go out on Sunset Way," he said. "You can read your instructions on the road out."

" 'Bye," she said softly.

" 'Bye," Jerry Bane said, and assisted her into the taxicab, then slammed the door. . . .

Jerry Bane found Mugs Magoo seated in the kitchen of the apartment, holding a newspaper propped up with one arm.

"Mugs," he said, "what would you do if you suddenly found yourself in possession of a lot of stolen jewelry?"

"That depends," Mugs said, looking up from the paper and regarding Jerry Bane with expressionless eyes.

"Depends on what?"

"On whether you wanted to be real smart or only half smart."

"I'd want to be *real* smart, Mugs."

"The point is," Mugs went on, "that if the jewelry is real hot, you'd have to fence it to sell it. If it was stuff that had cooled off a bit, it would be a great temptation to try passing off a little here and there. Either way would be half smart."

"And to be *real* smart, Mugs?"

"You'd get in touch with the insurance companies. You'd suggest to them that you *might* be able to help them make restorations here and there but you'd want it handled in such a way that you collected a reward."

"Would they pay?"

"If you make the right approach."

"How much?"

"If they thought they were dealing with a crook who was a squealer, they wouldn't pay very much. If they thought they were dealing with a reputable detective who had made a recovery, they'd come through pretty handsomely."

Bane reached in his pocket, took out a knotted handkerchief, untied the knots and let Magoo's eyes feast on the assorted collection of sparklers.

"Gosh!" Mugs Magoo said.

"I want to be *real* smart, Mugs."

"Okay," Mugs said, scooping up the handkerchief in his big hand. "I guess I know the angles. . . . Somebody going to miss this stuff?"

"I'm afraid so," Jerry Bane said, "but I think I juggled the inventory. Someone else may get part of it, Mugs. A selfish, greedy someone who may be only *half* smart."

Magoo regarded his friend with eyes that were cold with cynicism. "If this is what I think it is, this other guy will find the underworld can stick together like two pieces of flypaper. If he tries to chisel, he might even wind up pushing up daisies."

Jerry said, "Of course, if he's *really* honest, he'll report to the cops."

"Do you think he will be?"

"No."

"Okay," Mugs said. "Let him lead with *his* chin. We'll work undercover."

Jerry Bane was stretched out in the easy chair, a highball glass at his elbow, when timid knuckles tapped on the door of the apartment.

Mugs Magoo opened the door.

Bernice Calhoun said, "Oh, good evening. I *do* hope Mr. Bane is home. I have to see him. I—why, you're the man who—"

"He's home," Mugs Magoo said. "Come in."

Jerry Bane was getting to his feet as she entered the room. She ran to him and gave him both her hands. "Mr. Bane," she said, "the most *wonderful* thing has happened! I simply can't understand it."

"Sit down and tell me about it," Jerry said. "What do you want—Scotch or bourbon?"

"Scotch and soda."

Jerry nodded to Mugs Magoo, then said, "All right, Bernice, what happened?"

She said, "I didn't like the lawyer you took me to. He was very gruff. He asked a lot of questions and then said he'd go down to the grocery store and look the place over, but he didn't think he'd be particularly interested in the case. He didn't seem at all eager, not even cordial."

"And what happened?"

She said, "Well, after he'd asked a lot of questions, he went down to the store with me. I opened up and showed him just where I had been standing and all that. Then he looked around and asked a few questions and looked the shelves over, and I remembered what you'd told me and I tagged right along with him, and that seemed to irritate him. He made several attempts to get rid of me, but I stayed right beside him."

"Then what?" Jerry asked.

"Then a young woman came in. She was a very theatrical young woman with lots of makeup. She said rather loudly that she had been having a hard time getting the brand of dog food her dog wanted and that she noticed I had a stock of that brand. She asked me if she could buy my entire stock and if I'd take her check. She said her name was Stella Darling."

"Then what happened?" Jerry asked.

"The *strangest* thing," she said. "This lawyer advised me

to take no one's personal check, and he went back to the telephone and called his office."

"Go on," Jerry said.

"Well, it seemed that right while he was telephoning a client was in his office. This client had been looking for some small business that he could go into, something that he could operate on a one-man basis. I'd been telling Mr. Anson that I'd really like to sell out that grocery-store business, lock, stock and barrel, and—well, one thing led to another, and Mr. Anson negotiated over the telephone, and I sold the business right there."

"What did you do about an inventory?" Jerry flashed a glance at Mugs Magoo.

"Mr. Anson gave me his check, based on my own figures, and took immediate possession."

"And this Miss Darling who wanted to buy the dog food? Did the lawyer sell it to her?"

"Indeed, he did not. He literally put her out of the store, took the keys and locked up."

There was a moment of silence.

"And so," she said, "I—I wanted to thank you—personally."

The telephone rang, and Jerry picked it up.

Arthur Arman Anson's voice came over the wire. "Jerry, my boy, I've been doing a little thinking. After all, you're young, and I suppose the war rather upset your whole life. I think a man must make allowances for youth."

"Thank you, sir."

"I've covered the overdraft at your bank and deposited a few hundred dollars, Jerry, my boy. But try to be a little more careful with money."

"Yes, sir. Thank you, I will."

"And, Jerry, in case you should see Miss Calhoun, the young woman who had the grocery store, be very careful not to mention anything about that perfectly cockeyed theory you had. There was absolutely nothing to it."

"There wasn't?"

"No, my boy. I went down there and looked the place over. I inspected the can which the photograph shows was partially turned. It was just the same as any other can— nothing in it but dog food. However, it happened a client of mine was interested in a property such as Miss Calhoun has there and I was able to arrange a sale for her."

"Oh, that's splendid!" Jerry said.

"Purely a matter of business," Anson observed. "I was glad it worked out the way it did, because this young woman is very vulnerable to a lawsuit. She'd better get out of the state before papers can be served. As an ethical lawyer, I didn't want to tell her to do that, but in case you should see her, *you* can tell her to get out of the state at once. Get me?"

"Meaning I haven't your high ethics to handicap me?" Jerry asked.

"Very few men could live up to my ethics," Anson declared.

"Yes, I presume so. Very well, I'll tell her. You think she should get out of the state?"

"Yes, on a trip. At once."

"I'll tell her."

"Well, I won't keep you up any longer," Anson said.

"Keep me up!" Jerry laughed. "Is it by any chance bedtime?"

"Well, it's after ten o'clock," Arthur Anson said. "Good night, Jerry."

"Good night."

Jerry hung up the phone and turned to Bernice Calhoun. "Under the circumstances," he said, "don't you think we should do some dinner dancing?"

"Well," she told him demurely, "I came to thank you—"

Mugs said, "Did you by any chance hear the news on the radio, sir?"

Jerry Bane looked up quickly. "Should I?"

"I think you should have, sir."

"What was it?"

Mugs glanced at Bernice Calhoun.

"Go ahead," Jerry said. "She'll learn about it sooner or later."

"This man Gordon she had arrested," Mugs said, "was released from jail. He was being held on investigation and he dug up some bail. He was released about an hour ago."

"Indeed," Jerry said.

"And," Mugs went on, "the police are somewhat mystified. A witness told them that as Gordon walked down the jail steps, a car was waiting for him and a man said, 'Get in.' Gordon acted as though he didn't want to get in. He hesitated perceptibly, but finally got in the car. The witness felt certain a man in the back seat was holding a gun on Gordon. He was so certain of it that he went to the police to report, but there wasn't much the police could do about it. The license number on the automobile was spotted with mud and the man hadn't been able to get it."

"Oh," Bernice said, "then that man must have been connected with the underworld after all! Why do you suppose they wanted him to—to go for a ride?"

"Probably," Mugs Magoo said, "they wanted to get some information out of him. And with all night at their disposal, they'll quite probably get the information they want."

His eyes were significant as he looked steadily at Jerry Bane.

Bane stretched his arms and yawned. "Oh, well," he said, "tomorrow's a new day for all of us, and my friend, Arthur Anson, has bought Bernice's grocery store."

Bernice said, "I'm *so* relieved. The lawyer promised me

that, as part of the deal on the store, he'd see that I was in-
demnified in case this man started any suit against me. Now
that I've sold the store, I feel I haven't any responsibilities."

"That's just the way with me," Jerry Bane said. "Not a
care in the world! Let's go dance, baby."